MUGGER'S DAY

By George Bagby

MUGGER'S DAY
I COULD HAVE DIED
GUARANTEED TO FADE
BETTER DEAD
THE TOUGH GET GOING
INNOCENT BYSTANDER
MY DEAD BODY
TWO IN THE BUSH
KILLER BOY WAS HERE
HONEST RELIABLE CORPSE
ANOTHER DAY—ANOTHER
   DEATH
CORPSE CANDLE
DIRTY POOL
MYSTERIOUSER AND
   MYSTERIOUSER
MURDER'S LITTLE HELPER
EVIL GENIUS
THE REAL GONE GOOSE
THE THREE-TIME LOSERS
DEAD WRONG
COP KILLER
DEAD STORAGE
A DIRTY WAY TO DIE
THE BODY IN THE BASKET
DEAD DRUNK

GIVE THE LITTLE CORPSE A
   GREAT BIG HAND
THE CORPSE WITH STICKY
   FINGERS
SCARED TO DEATH
DEATH AIN'T COMMERCIAL
BLOOD WILL TELL
COFFIN CORNER
DROP DEAD
IN COLD BLOOD
THE STARTING GUN
THE TWIN KILLING
THE ORIGINAL CARCASE
DEAD ON ARRIVAL
MURDER CALLING "50"
RED IS FOR KILLING
HERE COMES THE CORPSE
THE CORPSE WORE A WIG
THE CORPSE WITH THE
   PURPLE THIGHS
BIRD WALKING WEATHER
MURDER ON THE NOSE
MURDER HALF-BAKED
RING AROUND A MURDER
MURDER AT THE PIANO
BACHELORS' WIFE

MUGGER'S DAY

GEORGE BAGBY

PUBLISHED FOR THE CRIME CLUB BY

DOUBLEDAY & CO., INC.

GARDEN CITY, NEW YORK

1979

All of the characters in this book are
fictitious, and any resemblance to ac-
tual persons, living or dead, is purely
coincidental.

ISBN:-0-385-15421-6
Library of Congress Catalog Card Number 79-7326
Copyright © 1979 by Doubleday & Company, Inc.
All Rights Reserved
Printed in the United States of America
First Edition

For
Adam John Horner
with love

MUGGER'S DAY

I.

I shouldn't have done it and I can't pretend that I didn't know better. I was touched and I was curious and I was outraged. As a result of all that, I was stupid. Inspector Schmidt is what you might call a business associate, but he is a friend as well. The inspector, in case you don't know, is the New York Police Department's Chief of Homicide. Whenever a case comes his way that is worth writing about, he has me do the writing.

Mostly it is early on in a case, if not at the very outset, that Schmitty senses this is going to be one that will have a story in it for me. Over the years it has become standard procedure on such investigations for him to call me in and keep me at his side until he has the case pinned down.

This one went the other way around. I scented a story and I pulled the inspector into it; and, as I say, it was something I shouldn't have done since Schmitty, after all, is Homicide, and when I brought it to him, it was standing far short of murder.

I'd been having lunch with the inspector and I had just dropped him off at his office down in headquarters. It happened to be one of those times when he had nothing coming across his desk but administrative routine, so there'd been no reason for my hanging on down there through the afternoon. I had just come out of headquarters and was crossing Police Plaza, heading for home. If you haven't been down that way recently and you are thinking of the old Center Street building, I'd better fill you in on Police

Plaza. Headquarters is now in a splendid new building with a broad open space in front of it. A wide stone parapet flanks this open space and separates it from one of the Brooklyn Bridge entrance ramps. About ten feet in from the parapet the plaza is ornamented by a large abstract sculpture. It is only when I am under the greatest stress that I can walk through there without pausing to admire the great view of the bridge and to enjoy the sculpture.

That afternoon I was under no stress, but there was something afoot in the plaza that drew my attention away from both. Over by the parapet there was this guy. He stood six foot seven or eight. He had the build and the carriage of an offensive linebacker. He had hair the color and sheen of burnished bronze and he wore it as though he'd have thought it indecent exposure to have allowed anyone to catch even a glimpse of his eyebrows, his ears, or the back of his neck. He also had a mustache you could hang your hat on and a spreading fan of burnished bronze beard. The beard curtained his Adam's apple as the hair of his head curtained his nape.

In his arms he had a baby. At his feet a creeper, still too small ever to have been up off all fours, seemed to be trying to get the guy's big toe into his mouth. This hirsute Goliath was wearing sandals, so the big toe was available, and it was big. There was too much of it. The kid had a small mouth. A pair of toddlers were at the behemoth's knee, and out of even his impressive reach a couple of free spirits were exploring. They had found the sculpture. One small boy had climbed it and was fence-walking its top. Since he was negotiating it with great determination and neither skill nor balance, disaster was imminent. The other of that pair was climbing up to join him. It was obvious that he was going to fall before he'd even made it to the top.

Turning to look at me, the balancer promptly unbalanced. I reached out and caught him before he hit the stone pavement. With my free hand I plucked the other one off the sculpture. I was trying to set them on their feet, but that was where they didn't want to be. They were bent on fighting their way back to the challenge of that sculpture. The one I'd grabbed with my left hand was a handful. The other was a wildcat.

The keeper of the flock didn't move from the parapet. There wasn't much he could have done in the way of moving without dumping the baby and treading on the other three tots. He didn't seem to mind being immobilized. Content to let me handle what I had picked up, he left it at offering advice.

"In your left hand," he said, "you've got Terry. It takes only a few seconds for him to run down. Keep a good, firm grip on him and pretty soon he'll stop flailing around. You've got to wait that long before he'll listen, but you can reason with Terry."

Just on the behavior of the other of the pair, I could have guessed, but these instructions eliminated guesswork: they carried the obvious implication that what I had in my right hand would be beyond reason. I made the inference. I have a good fielding average on implications.

"How do I handle the wildcat?" I asked. "Handcuffs, or does it take a straitjacket?"

"They don't make them small enough," Big Shaggy answered. "He'll slip right out of the cuffs, and to begin to fill a straitjacket, you'd have to stuff the rest of them in with him and that wouldn't be right because they're sane. The wildcat's Jack. He's more of a problem."

"Your problem, mister, not mine. I'm not keeping him."

"Sure enough you're not. No way. But for right now you've got him and I can't take him off your hands because

I've got the baby and you're handling Jack all right while I've got to get this baby changed pretty quick. So unless you know your way around a diaper . . . "

"Way around," I said. "Nowhere near."

"I thought as much. You better keep Jackie, but watch it. The state he's in now, he's like a bull terrier who's been too long away from his psychiatrist. Given half a chance, he bites and with ferocity yet. Hang on to him the way you are but stay out of reach of his teeth."

"How long does it take him to run down?"

As promised, Terry had subsided. If I could have worked out any sort of detachment from Jackie, I could even have begun reasoning with Terry.

"He never runs down. You have to turn him on to listening. It's done by smacking him. One good stinger on the seat of his pants is all it takes. Jackie is programmed for it. It tunes him in. Then you can talk to him."

I was tempted, but I controlled myself.

"This," I said, "is Police Plaza. We're under the eye of New York's finest. There's a law against assault and that could include planting stingers on the seat of a citizen's pants."

Gargantua laughed.

"That's a citizen?" he asked. "You don't have to whack him so hard that he'll remember it all the way till he's old enough to vote."

"They've lowered the age," I said. "Also I don't have to whack him at all. I can just let go of him. He'll climb back up where he was. He'll fall off and smack himself against the paving stones. I can't guarantee it will be exactly where you want it, but he will get hurt."

"Could you just hang on to him and bring him within range?"

"That I can do," I said.

I moved the kid within reach. Shifting the baby to a one-handed grip, Big and Bushy freed the other hand for tuning Jackie in. It took only one surprisingly moderate whack and both handfuls were in shape for the reasoning process. He took that on as well and with admirable brevity. All he did was tell them to behave themselves or he'd trade them to Kansas City for a couple of outfielders.

Having disposed of that piece of business, he turned to me.

"I came down here thinking I maybe could talk to some top cop. I've wasted my time. You look important. Can I talk to you?"

I looked at the kids.

"I'm not important," I said, "but I can tell you this much. The police aren't likely to deal with them, not even on a juvenile-delinquency basis. And besides you're doing all right with them. Maybe you've overextended yourself. If you took them just two at a time ... "

"I take them the way they come," the Jolly Giant said. "It's always this way in large lots. Where do we go to talk?"

"What do we talk about?"

"Mothers' Day. Ripoffs."

Catching the first of that, I sidetracked myself in the calendar.

"It's been and gone. It's almost a year before it comes around again."

I had the man diagnosed for a nut, and the best way to handle nuts is to play along with them in the hope of finding the right word for easing yourself away from them.

"You're promising another ripoff? Is that all you can do?"

"You've been ripped off? Have you taken your story to your local precinct?"

"To both questions: I haven't. The precinct fuzz I've had up to here."

He indicated mustache level. He could have been punning, but he wasn't.

"If you haven't been ripped off, who has?"

The big guy indicated his platoon of charges.

"Their mom," he said.

"Your wife?"

"No such luck. I'm just the baby-sitter."

"Since she has a baby-sitter, why isn't she making her own complaint?"

"One: because they put her in the hospital, two: because she'd think it an exercise in futility. She's probably right, but I'm checking it out before I go on the warpath myself, which will mean doing what in your language is called murder."

"What's it called in your language?"

"Need we have a name for it? How about sanitation? For now I'll call it that. If I think of something better, I may let you know."

"Okay," I said. "Let's see if there's anything I can do for you."

See what I mean? This was where I stepped out of line. There was very little likelihood that I could do anything for him, and I knew as much. Since nobody had been murdered and since even the big lug's threat of murder impressed me as no more than a bit of all too common hyperbole, his complaint was out of Inspector Schmidt's territory. Furthermore, I knew the inspector too well to think that he could easily be induced to invade a fellow-officer's turf. He's always been dead set against that kind of interference. It doesn't make for good departmental relations.

But, as I said, I was touched by the kids, curious about

their gargantuan baby-sitter, and outraged by what he was telling me. One would like to think that every policeman does his job and that there is no precinct anywhere in the city that is corruptible, but unhappily you can't count on it. I wanted the inspector to hear this character's story. It could be that there was a precinct that needed something drastic done about it. I was aware that it would not be within the inspector's direct power to do anything about it, but Schmitty is not without weight in the NYPD. He might put the right word in the right ear.

I started back toward headquarters and I watched Big and Bushy shape up his troops for the march inside. Still holding the baby in a one-handed grip, he reached down with the free hand and scooped up the little one he'd had at his feet. The child seemed to take the move with equanimity. Deprived of the big toe, he was obviously happy enough to be raised to a level where he might aspire toward ingesting a mouthful of hair-mantled ear.

With a kid on each arm, the oversized baby-sitter was, of course, fresh out of hands. It was evident, however, that he had been in that situation before. He knew how to deal with it.

"Fall in, gang," he barked, putting into it the best parade-ground rasp. "Column of whatsis, march!"

The pair I had hauled down from the sculpture turned out to be surprisingly well drilled. Each one pulled up alongside one of the toddlers and together they took charge. Taking grubby little fists into their not much larger and no less grubby paws, they pulled the little ones along, bringing their charges and themselves neatly to heel. That evidently was column of whatsis. It was impressive.

I rang Schmitty from the lobby and gave him a quick fill-in on what I'd had from the big guy. He said it would be okay to bring them up to his office, reminding me the while

not to expect he'd be able to do much. During the time I was on the phone, my big friend was even more impressive. He kept those kids in line.

Up in the inspector's office, however, he was most impressive. Subjecting Schmitty's desk to a quick inspection, my new buddy marched on it. Schmitty keeps a desk top as neat and unencumbered as his mind. Lowering the toddler to the floor where he could again be happily occupied with that big toe, the big guy set the baby down on the desk. It took him only a moment to break the rest of his troops out of marching formation and give them their orders.

"Sit," he told them, "and stay sat. First man up on his feet gets a leg pulled off. First man who touches anything loses a hand. Dig?"

They dug. Schmitty didn't have near enough chairs to go around and they couldn't have made it up into such chairs as he had unless they were lifted, but they didn't try for chairs. They just dropped where they had been standing and settled themselves in a cross-legged row on the floor. Slung from his shoulder by a canvas strap big boy had a canvas bag. He dropped it on the desk alongside the baby and produced from it five toy pistols which he distributed to his five small squatters.

"Water pistols," he explained, "but unloaded." Turning to the baby, he explained him as well. "This fellow isn't loaded either," he said, "since he's only just after unloading into his diaper. I'll have him changed in a sec and then we can get down to stuff."

He came close to being as good as his word. All of the necessaries came out of his canvas bag. Neither Schmitty nor I have any expert knowledge of diaper changing, but if the job has ever been done with greater speed and efficiency, we'll have to be shown. The way this guy performed, we could well have entered him in the Olympics.

He was as neat as he was quick, stowing all his equipment away in the canvas bag. When he had finished, found himself a chair, and settled himself in it with the baby cradled in his lap, he had left the desk exactly as he'd found it, with never a trace of the purpose to which he had put it.

"That's it," he said. "Ready to listen?"

"Ready to talk?" Inspector Schmidt asked.

"Suppose we begin with some questions I have bothering me," I said. "You say their mother is in the hospital. You say she was the victim of a Mothers' Day ripoff. It put her in the hospital and we have to assume she's been there ever since. That's a long time without a squawk. Where have you been up to now and why now? ·

He shrugged.

"Long time, short time," he said. "What difference? A sweet kid, who's got troubles enough even without anybody leaning on her, doesn't need anybody half killing her. She also doesn't need a society that won't get off its ass to do anything more than tut-tut even if it should go all the way. What do you want to know? What happened or how quick I made it down here from the hospital?"

"We know how quick," I said right back to him. "More than a month."

Even though the eyebrows were hidden under the bangs, I could guess that one of them did a quizzical lift. There was the compensatory shift in the parts of his face left out in the open.

"More than a month? Since this morning more than a month?"

"Since Mothers' Day. You operate a calendar of your own?"

He looked disgusted enough to spit.

"That," he said, "is the Mothers' Day of the middle

class. The establishment carnation in the establishment buttonhole. These men and their mom don't have any carnations. They're lucky to have buttonholes. Where they live Mothers' Day means something different."

"The day the welfare payments come through for the mothers with dependent children?"

Inspector Schmidt put the question as though he wanted to be enlightened. He'll do that to ease me out of a corner, pretending that he's been as ignorant as I was.

"And that was this morning," the big baby-sitter said.

So it was the all too familiar story. The public-assistance checks go out in the mail. The public-assisted mothers go downstairs early. They wait by their letter boxes in the tenement hallways and they watch for the letter carrier. They are there to snatch the envelope before it has even dropped into the box. They know all there is to know about stolen welfare checks and forged endorsements.

They hurry straight down the street to a local check-cashing service. With the money tucked down in her bosom, the welfare mother rushes back home. Like the salmon fighting their way upstream, not all of them make it. In the darker recesses of the tenement halls the ripoff artists lie in wait. They know their way down into the bosoms.

Sometimes it takes no more than intimidation. Sometimes it will be one of the standard holdup techniques: a knife, an icepick, a gun. Any of these might come into play or it may be punching or kicking or stomping or strangling. Whatever the method and whatever the degree of violence, it's robbery.

"Never a time it doesn't happen," the big boy said. "It's their regular Mothers' Day thing, as American as apple pie. A mother has nothing to go on but a prayer that in her

building it won't be the day that it's her turn to take the hit."

It seemed to me that he was making the process sound too neatly organized.

"You trying to tell us that the muggers take them in rotation?" I asked.

"They don't care how they take them. It's the smash-and-grab deal."

"The bigger the family," Schmitty added, "the fatter the welfare check. They might let a mother or two go by if they know it's only one or two kids. They might wait for bigger pickings. Given a shot at the mother of this many men, they'll never pass her up."

"That's it," our informant said. "She's just got to be lucky."

He outlined for us the components of a welfare mother's luck. It had to be that some other mother in the building had come through the halls before her.

"A sonofabitch does one," he said, "and then he can't hang on in the building to rip off another. He has to lam out of there. It's all in the luck of the timing. This time it hit their mom. This time her luck ran out."

"Hospital?" I said. "How bad is it?"

"A couple of cracked ribs, and they're watching for internal injuries. She took some heavy boot stuff in the belly."

"Of course, she tried to fight it," the inspector said.

"Your buddy here handled Jack and Terry. You can look at Mike and Jimmy." Their baby-sitter indicated the two toddlers. "And Dickie." He used his beslobbered big toe to indicate the mite who was still engaged with that imposing member. "Not to speak of Danny even though he's asleep right now and that might fool you because they all look this mild when they are sleeping." He was holding the

baby up for us to see. It did look a cherub. "Look at these guys," he urged, "and you tell me whether the lady who produced them and is getting them raised up is likely to be anything but a fighter."

I was looking at the six of them. It was obvious that she had started with twins, Jack and Terry. Second time around it had been twins again, Mike and Jimmy. With Dickie and Danny she had evidently sloped down to single births; but, even figuring it at four deliveries, I couldn't work it out for anything but the closest possible spacing.

"More than a fighter," I said, "a baby-making assembly line. She didn't even pause for station identification."

"That, mister, is her business. Until they pass a law against it, it'll never be any of yours."

"Where's the father?" Schmitty asked.

Mine had been a comment. An argument could have been made for calling it irrelevant. Inspector Schmidt's was a question, and I couldn't see where anyone would rate it as being much off the mark. Big and Bushy didn't agree.

"Also her business," he said. "None of mine and I mind my own."

"You also mind her kids," Schmitty said.

"I do what's necessary. Humiliating people is not one of my necessities."

The inspector grinned at him.

"If you dropped by, my friend, to parade your nobility, you've made your point. We're impressed. You're great with a diaper, maybe the fastest safety pin in town, and you're sickeningly pure in heart. But if the idea was to give information that could possibly help her or even help us, then, brother, you're nowhere."

"The idea was to satisfy myself that she's right when she thinks she can expect no more from you guys than all the

other ripped-off mothers have ever had from the cops—to whit: one great, big, fat minus quantity."

"So give us nothing we can get started with," the inspector told him, "and you take no risk of not satisfying yourself. Are there any questions you'd consider answering?"

"Reasonable ones."

"And it's you who judges what's reasonable?"

"Since I can't consult with them," he said, indicating the troops. "They're still too young."

"Ripoff this morning," the inspector said. "Your local precinct has been informed?"

"The cops come with the ambulance. You're an emergency in this town, you can't get to the hospital without having to climb over them."

"Her name?"

"Norah Simms."

"Mrs. or Miss?"

"Ms."

He didn't have to label it an unreasonable question. His answer carried the implication. Schmitty took it as it came. He wasn't pushing.

"Address?" he asked.

Our unfriendly volunteer supplied it. To anyone who knows the distribution of the local pestholes, it was nothing unexpected. It wasn't on the street that had been labeled the worst block on Manhattan, but it was in an area that lacked only the label. The label, in case you don't know, was pinned on that other street by a crusading clergyman who happened to adopt the block as his special province and whose faith in publicity may have been surpassed only by his faith in God.

"Time she was hit?"

"Nine-thirty—maybe a couple of minutes before or a couple after. She has no watch and she didn't have one

even before. Also it's a dark hall, and they don't give you time for scratching matches and squinting at faces, not watch faces and not their faces."

"Nine-thirty, give or take a few minutes," the inspector said. "That's close enough. The next question I guess you've already answered. She saw no one?"

"In the dark, hit without warning and from behind."

"Always the same," Schmitty said.

I knew what was bugging him. We know those halls. Only occasionally are they as dark as people say they are. None of them blaze with light, but most of them are not the back side of the moon. Go looking for a witness to anything that happens in one of those halls, however, and you come up against an epidemic of night blindness. Nobody can ever see anything, and who's to sort out which in truth couldn't see, which were afraid to see, and which for reasons of their own chose not to see.

"Always the same," the big baby-sitter agreed, but he had a comment with which to temper his agreement. "And always the same questions," he added, "neatly designed for building a case against trying to do anything about it."

The inspector let that one shoot past him.

"Anything toward an identification?" he asked. "A voice she might recognize? Something she felt? Smelled? Sensed in any way?"

"They don't talk. They're all slimy, and all of them stink."

"Then you'd say she could give us nothing?"

"Nothing. That's the point. If it was just a matter of dealing with him, who'd need you? It's a matter of finding him, and we're asked to believe the official mythology that says you are the ones who have the means."

"Not when we get no cooperation."

"She cooperated. She tried to collar him for you. What more do you want?"

"A lot more," Inspector Schmidt said, "and a lot less."

The big boy made an elaborate show of ignoring the first of that.

"I can go with less," he said. "So what do you want?"

"Witnesses. Anybody who can give us even the slightest lead. Were you around? Did you see anything? Strangers hanging around the building? Somebody coming in? Somebody running out?"

"I was upstairs riding herd on these kids and a dozen more. The mothers go for their money. They pool the kids and leave them with me. I was no place where I could see anything. I couldn't even hear when she yelled for help. You're letting eighteen kids have themselves a time. You don't hear anything past that."

"She yelled for help?"

"I'm guessing she did. Wouldn't she?"

"Anybody hear her? The neighbors? Other women?"

That question drew the inspector a laugh. You know the kind. It has nothing to do with mirth and everything to do with scorn.

"The way they live," our know-nothing informant said, "they take care not to see anything and not to hear anything."

"I can't make any promises, but I'll check it out with precinct," the inspector said. "We'll need your name."

"Dan Mallard."

"Occupation?"

"Actor."

"Work nights and baby-sit days?"

"Work when I can get it."

"But now at liberty?"

"I call it unemployed."

"Meaning that you're collecting your unemployment?"

"No business of yours, but no."

"No business of mine, but why not?"

"Ever heard of residuals?"

"TV?"

Mallard nodded. "Commercials," he said. "And if you're wondering why you can't remember ever seeing me, forget it. Nobody knows me with my shirt on. They never use me —only the muscles."

"Your address?"

"The same."

"Same as what?"

Mallard indicated the six little boys.

"Same as theirs."

Nothing passed between the inspector and me. We took it dead pan. Our shaggy visitor, however, assumed it was there.

"If the way you get your kicks is from thinking I'm shacked up with their ma," he said, "I've got to spoil your fun. I'm not that lucky. It's a tenement, and a tenement is a broken-down multiple dwelling where a lot of households struggle along independently. They have their roach run. I have mine. Same floor. They're the front. I'm the rear."

Inspector Schmidt laughed.

"You said it," he said. "We didn't."

The big boy took a moment to get that one clear in his head. I'd caught it before it bounced, and I wondered what the inspector thought he was building. If he wanted to know whether the muscles were for anything more than show, it seemed a good way to find out. Mallard, however, who had repeatedly demonstrated his capacity for coming up with a hostile reaction to nothing at all, now showed not even a flash of resentment. He took it with a laugh.

"I'm the rear," he repeated. "Right. From where you sit

I've got to be an asshole. I come down here with nothing but my rage and helplessness and frustration and I blow it all off on you. What can you do? What can anybody do? So I flipped and I've been wasting your time. Is it any use my telling you it's done me a lot of good? I feel better for it."

"Don't expect the feeling to last," Schmitty said. "I choke on frustration all the time."

"One more thing to choke on," Mallard said. "These rip-offs—we hear about them all over the neighborhood and it's always been two guys working as a pair. In our hall they hit oftener than anywhere else and any time they've hit there, it's been like that, the two guys. This morning, Norah says it was only one. She's mad at herself even. Because it was only one, she thinks she should have been able to handle him."

"A new operator taking over the territory," I said, thinking aloud.

"Or an added menace," Mallard suggested. "Twice now what there had been where there's always been more than enough. Other places around the neighborhood a mother gets hit in one building or another. In our dump it's every time. Where we live they never miss a Mothers' Day."

"That's a record you can do without," the inspector said.

"And how? Who needs the honor of living in the worst house in town?"

I knew it was wildly irrelevant, but in this era of good feeling I thought I might try to satisfy my curiosity.

"The police can't get away from it," I said. "It's their job. They're stuck with it, but are you? On those residuals, surely you could live in some other kind of place."

"In another kind of place you find another kind of people, and I don't like them much. I'm where I belong, with the kind of people I like—these men, their mom, all the kids, all the moms."

II.

The inspector carried through on his promise. He did check it out with precinct. It happened that he could do so without moving officially, which was just as well since he didn't have nearly enough for initiating any official moves in his capacity as Chief of Homicide. There aren't many precincts around the city where Schmitty can't make a connection with some buddy he worked with one time or another. For the address Mallard had given us, however, the inspector was specially well connected. The precinct captain was Wishes Leary, and the friendship went all the way back to when they'd been rookie cops and together had been assigned to their first duty. Leary's nickname also went back to that same time of first duty.

Leary was a good cop, sensible, sensitive, honest, and with all the warmth and generosity it takes if a man is to confront the ugliness and the evil that comes the way of any cop and still retain the sense of mission that makes him want to understand and to help. You can accept Inspector Schmidt's judgment of the man. He was the kind of cop the people need, but he was also the kind of cop who would seldom get through a day's tour of duty without breaking his heart.

But why Wishes? On that first assignment the two rookies were platooned with an older officer called Al Leary. Two Al Learys in one platoon would cause confusion, but even the parents who fasten on a boy the name of Aloysius don't on any day-to-day basis use all of it. Since the first of

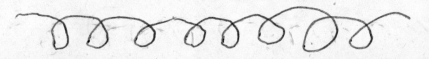

these two Learys, therefore, was already called Al, the second had to make do with the closing syllables—Wishes.

The inspector phoned him and I hooked in on the call. Wishes knew Norah Simms. He knew her kids. He also knew Dan Mallard.

"There's two days a month every month," Wishes said, "when I know I'm going to touch bottom. I wake up those days and I've got to fight myself. I get it that bad wanting to call in sick. I have to kick myself into my pants and kick myself down to the station house. This is one of my two days, Schmitty."

"And the other one will also be Mothers' Day."

"Sure thing. It's not that these ripoffs are the worst things that come at us. I could give you a catalogue to curl your hair and it's not like you haven't seen your share of the mean ones. What eats me specially about these is the way they come on schedule, like they're built into the system."

"Aren't they?" I asked.

"Of course they are, Baggy. Look, guys. Can we get together and talk about it? I've been yelling. I'd like to get you yelling with me. Somebody's got to light a fire under the welfare people or whoever. There's got to be a change in the way they make the payments."

We made a date to pick him up for dinner that evening. Since Inspector Schmidt was flexible, Wishes set the time. The inspector had a long office day, but Leary's was longer. When we pulled out, it was still early for the time Wishes had set.

"Time enough for visiting the sick," the inspector suggested.

"Norah Simms? Mallard says she's a cop hater and Wishes knows her. That means she holds out against

Leary's Irish charm. What makes you think you have a chance?"

"Wishes goes in with three strikes on him. He's the man on the spot. I'm big brass. That just might impress Ms. Simms."

I was laying bets it would be a waste of time, but I think Schmitty was taking it as an escape from administrative routine. I went along with him, expecting nothing. I was, however, curious to see the liberated woman who was that much a slave to childbearing.

So we stopped by the hospital. It's a good hospital even though it doesn't look it. The building is old and it carries a case load horrifyingly heavier than the space and the facilities should be called upon to handle. The staff, however, is as dedicated as it is able. Where it takes a miracle to cope at all, they knock themselves out for the double miracle of operating decently.

We checked with the floor nurse, expecting nothing more than directions to the right ward and the right bed. The odds were the nurse would be far too busy to stop for even a moment's chitchat. Just on first sight of her, as we stepped out of the elevator, I had her tabbed for one of the stiff-necked kind, the sort that with passionate rigidity hews to the letter of her professional ethics.

If you know hospitals at all, you know what I mean. These types are great with patients, but to the rest of the world they're the chilled steel battle-axes who'll only grudgingly give you a word of any kind and never under any circumstances a word of gossip.

We introduced ourselves. What had begun as a chill snapped down to a flash freeze. You could feel what she was thinking. Visitors were the last thing any patient needed. Visitors broke into a patient's rest. Even doctors

would at best be a necessary evil. Patients did best when left entirely to her. Everybody else disturbed them.

Just on that the temperature had been frosty. The word that we were from Police Headquarters sent it down past the freezing point. If ordinary visitors were bad for a patient, police visitors were poison. The calmest of patients, one who was doing fine, need be exposed to a police officer, if only for a few minutes, and he would be left a quivering wreck who'd have to be put on sedation. Out of her deepest glacial fissures she fetched up a sigh.

"There isn't a patient here well enough to be worried by anyone," she said. "That, of course, will make no difference to you."

Cranking up the charm, Inspector Schmidt shoved it into top gear. His smile melted nothing. His words drew from her no more than a look of stubborn disbelief.

"To us it'll make all the difference," he said. "We won't go near her if you feel it's better not."

"Of course, it's better not."

"Norah Simms? We thought it might do her some good to know we cared, just the indication that we're on it."

"And high time too," our embattled Florence Nightingale said. "Now that it's murder."

"Norah Simms?" I exclaimed. "Rib fractures and, even with the possibility of internal injuries, you haven't been carrying her as critical or anything like that."

"Norah, poor child. She's doing well enough. It's the baby. She's miscarried. Four times everything perfect right straight through the pregnancy. Four times the easiest kind of delivery, even the twice it was the twins. This was going to be as good a one as ever and she's lost it."

I can't pretend I didn't have the thought that on the lady's track record it might be assumed that there always could be more. Carefully I put that thought away. I wasn't

going to let any hint of it show. We were benefiting from an unlooked-for thaw in the nurse's hostility. We had touched a soft spot. Norah Simms wasn't just another patient. For this dame Norah Simms seemed to be special.

It wasn't only that on nothing more than the mention of Norah's name the nurse had softened. She was babbling, and much of her babble was down at gossip level.

If it hadn't been for the miscarriage, she might not have even known Norah Simms had been injured. On rib fractures alone there might easily have not been a hospital admission.

"Cracked ribs," she said. "They wrap an ace bandage around her, give her some aspirin, let her rest a while down in emergency, and send her home."

It had been because of the possibility of internal injuries that a bed had been found for her and, since she'd been pregnant, it was a bed in this maternity section of the hospital. Maybe you're wondering how I could have been unaware of which section it was. I hadn't been unaware, but I knew too much of what's been happening in our overcrowded hospitals. They have an emergency. The proper ward is stuffed to capacity. If pressure has slacked off in some other section, you don't let departmental boundary lines stand in the way of filling an empty bed with this emergency you can't turn away.

I suppose it should have occurred to me that on her past record Ms. Simms might have been expected to be in production; but, with all Dan Mallard had to say about the dastardly act of attacking a mother of six, you'd think he might have mentioned the even more dastardly act of attacking the mother of a seventh in process.

Meanwhile, once uncorked, the floor nurse was running on and on. She protested that she was not the sort who

would permit herself to make pets of patients. At the least it would be unprofessional.

"Every woman comes on my ward gets the same treatment," she said. "For every last one of them I do the best I can. I'd be ashamed to do less, but they come and they go and your mind has to be on the one who's in the bed now. You can't be thinking about the one who had it yesterday. Not to speak of the ones we get here you're glad to forget."

"We can see Norah Simms isn't one of those," the inspector said.

Norah Simms was anything but one of those. It wasn't merely that she had been on the ward so often that just on frequency she'd be remembered. She was sweet as an angel, lovable as a baby, straight as an arrow, brave as a lion, honest as the day is long, and generous to a fault. If there is any cliché of praise omitted from the above catalogue, it will only be because it has slipped my mind. The nurse didn't miss a one. Eventually, however, she did run down and the inspector got a word in.

"You said she's doing well?"

I expected the quick about-face into telling us that Norah was still a very sick girl. Our nurse friend couldn't miss spotting Schmitty's question for a lead-in. Despite all her wildly out of character babble, she was too sharp and too much the old hand to miss out on that. Oddly she didn't react.

"She's doing beautifully. She always does. She's a strong kid and she's healthy, and with her character and temperament and courage she always does well. You can go in and talk to her, but wait here while I go in and see if she's awake. They hate to have strangers come in on them when there's a cheek all pillow-creased and the hair a mess."

She hurried off down the corridor and out of sight around a corner. I gave up on trying to predict her. I just

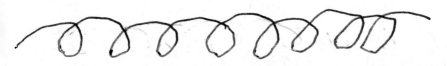

wondered what she'd come back with. She came back with a lump in her throat and a tear in her eye. Swallowing the one, she dashed the other away with the back of her hand.

"Give her a couple of minutes," she said, "then you can go in."

"You can tell us when," the inspector said. "She's not in the ward?"

There was a ward at the end of the corridor. We could see into it. Our nurse hadn't gone in there. She'd turned off short of it.

"I managed a small room for her where she can be alone. I wish I could do it for all of them when they lose a child, but we don't have the space. On the ward with the new mothers and watching when the babies are brought in for feeding—it's brutal, but what can we do?"

"What you've done," I said. "Get them out of there when you can."

She sighed. "It's not often I can." She paused a moment, looking down the corridor toward the ward, evidently thinking hard about something. Then quickly she came back to us. "You know," she said, "human nature's a funny thing. Norah now—when I think of all the times I talked to her and got nowhere."

She looked down the corridor again, this time just darting a quick glance in that direction but talking straight through without pause. She could have been trying to fix our attention so firmly on her words that we mightn't have noticed what her eyes were doing.

"The Pill," she said, "a diaphragm, a loop, everything available. She always listened. She always heard me out, but it was always the same. It wasn't for her. She loved her babies too much. She could never have too many."

She looked off down the corridor again. She could have been forgetting what she'd been saying.

The inspector reminded her.

"And now she's surprised you?"

"Yes. It's the last thing I'd have expected would come of her losing the baby. I suppose it's the first time she's felt it might not always be clear sailing. Maybe she's learned something about herself. She can lose a baby and it isn't the end of her world, or maybe it is the end of her world. I don't know. Maybe she can't bear the thought of its happening to her this way again. Better not to start one than to have it like this."

"She's changed her mind about the Pill?" I asked.

"No. She says that once she's come to it, she wants to be absolutely sure. As soon as she's over this and the doctors will do it, she's going to have her tubes tied off."

We were in visiting hours. All the time we'd been at her desk a trickle of husbands and other relatives had been going by. It was still early in the hours. Most of the traffic was on its way in. Occasionally someone would be heading out toward the elevators. It could be a man cutting his visit short because back home there were other kids who couldn't be left too long alone. Sometimes it would be just a matter of too many visitors around the one bed and early birds pulling out to give the late comers their turn.

A man came out of the ward and headed for the elevators. He caught my eye. He was an eye-catching sight. It was his looks and his carriage and it was the way he filled his tight knit shirt and his even tighter blue jeans. He was a startlingly handsome man, a beautiful head and a beautiful body, but you could think that he was unaware of his beauty. That wasn't what he was projecting. It was his virility. This was the human equivalent of the prize bull, of the wild stallion, and just walking that hospital corridor he was with his every move letting the world know it.

I suppose that sounds as though I were telling you the

man was strutting, that just in his passage down the corridor he was making a conscious display of his potential for sexual athleticism. He wasn't. Of that I was certain. If anything, I had the impression that he was trying to make his exit as inconspicuously as possible. He looked like a man who didn't want to be noticed, who would have been happy to be invisible. The aura of rampant sexuality he carried about with him was too much a part of him. He was incapable of shedding it.

Just as he was coming toward us, our loquacious nurse pulled up short. She might have been hit with a sudden realization of having said too much.

"We've given her more than enough time," she said. "I'll show you where she is."

Beckoning us to follow, she started off. We were headed for a face-to-face confrontation with the man I'd been noticing. He came to a quick stop. For a moment he looked as though he would dive back into the ward he had just left. Instead he dropped to one knee and ducked his head low while he fussed with his boot. He should have been wearing shoes. You can make a big thing out of untying and retying shoelaces, and who's to say they haven't been too tight? There isn't much you can do with an elastic-sided boot, nothing that will keep your head down for more than a moment or two. He did what he could. He took the boot off. He shook it. He peered into it and shook it again. You know how bits of gravel will take off from a tiled hospital floor to lodge themselves inside a man's boot.

It was enough to keep him down with his face out of sight until we had passed him and had turned out of the corridor. We were off in a small side hall when the inspector spoke of him. The man had caught Inspector Schmidt's attention just as he had mine. I was wondering whether the inspector was coming away from our glimpse of him with

the same impression as was bothering me. There was something familiar about the man's face. He resembled someone. I couldn't think who it might be. The inspector said nothing of that. He commented only on the fellow's behavior.

"You run this floor with an iron hand," he said, grinning at our guide.

"I run it for the patients. If I have to get tough, I get tough."

"Like with the guy we just passed in the corridor?"

"One of the visitors? What guy?"

"The one who was in a sweat to hit the elevator without tangling with you."

"Was there one? I didn't notice. New fathers celebrate in every bar along the street and they come in roaring drunk to visit the little woman. I make short work of them. Even after they've sobered up, they remember me."

She'd been leading the way along the little hall, but when the inspector had spoken to her, she'd stopped and turned to answer him. Now she jerked her thumb over her shoulder.

"She's down there," she said. "First door to your left. You can't miss it. Don't stay too long and don't upset her. You can have ten minutes, no more. If you're not out by then, I'll come and get you."

"We won't overstay," the inspector assured her. "And we're better than a tranquilizer. You'll see."

Laughing, she took off back to her desk. I'd had her pegged for the type that wouldn't laugh easily and whose laughs, when they did come, would be more likely to be derisive than mirthful. And now she was laughing with the inspector. For me his tranquilizer line didn't rate as a kneeslapper. The inspector and I went on toward the door she'd indicated.

"Was it a funny joke?" I asked. "It went right past me."

"Funny jokes don't bring hollow laughs," the inspector said. "That wasn't amusement. It was relief."

"Relief from what?"

"It'll be interesting to know."

The inspector turned in at the first door to our left.

Don't ask why I'd had it fixed in my mind that Norah Simms was going to be a great beauty. Nobody had said anything about her looks. I suppose it was her six great-looking kids. Would you expect a woman with a plain sort of face to mother a sextet of small Adonises? Norah was nobody's beauty. That's not to say she was a horror. She had what people call a nice face. People are inclined to take a liking to girls with these nice faces and, because they like the girl, they search her features for specifics they can praise. I could imagine people saying she had a fine, fair skin or that she had expressive eyes. She had a generous mouth, and that's another way of saying it was too wide and too full. Her chin was too firm. Her nose was too strong and proud.

If she had wanted time for prettying herself up, her buddy, the nurse, had given her more than enough. She could have put on some lipstick. She could have powdered her nose. She could have run a comb through her hair. She could have worked up something like a welcoming smile. Her lips were pale and they had a dry look. Her nose was shining. Her mouth was set in an angry line. She was scowling and her gaze was fiery. We came in and she didn't even look at us. She was too much occupied with her rage.

We introduced ourselves.

"Police Headquarters. You'll be the pair of big shots Dan Mallard talked to, or are you somebody they sent?"

"Mallard talked to us," I said.

"He exaggerates," the inspector added. "At best we're no more than a couple of medium-sized shots."

She almost smiled. I think she tried, but she couldn't quite bring it off. She was too much in no mood for smiling.

"What Dan says he told you, that's the whole thing. You've got to hear it again straight from me?"

"Straight from you, in complete detail," the inspector told her. "Every last thing you remember, whether you think it fits or not."

She did as the inspector asked but without any flicker of hope or show of interest. She was repeating to us what she had already told the precinct police. It was possible that it was also what she had told Dan Mallard. In any event it was precisely the story as we'd had it from Mallard, nothing more and nothing less. If there was anything further that she was choosing to hold back, she had either kept it from the baby-sitting behemoth or they had agreed between themselves that it was to remain their secret.

Probing for something more, the inspector questioned her, but to no avail.

"Ask around the house," she said. "Some of the girls will tell you it's the landlord."

"Is he that tough?" the inspector asked.

"He's an old man. His hands shake. They shake so bad, he can only just grab the rent. He couldn't mug a baby. He hasn't the strength, but they'll tell you he has some narco goons working for him and he splits with them, but that's only because nobody likes the landlord. Nobody likes you people either, so a lot of the girls say the cops are in on the take, too. They probably won't tell you that because you're from Police Headquarters, but they think it."

"How about you?" the inspector asked. "What do you think?"

She thought the police could do more to protect the mothers. She thought the landlord could do more toward lighting the halls.

"He could also fix the pipes and he could give more heat. He could maybe even do something about the rats and roaches. I'd like the old man better if he did some of these things, but do you think he's got something going where he splits with the rats and the roaches? I don't."

Our ten minutes was running out and, even though the formidable floor nurse hadn't come around to send us packing, we were coming up on the time when we had to be moving if we were going to keep our appointment with Wishes Leary.

"We'll see what we can do," the inspector said. "We're going to have a talk with Captain Leary. He says he knows you."

"Captain Leary? He'll tell you I beat up on myself and stole my own money."

"He told us you didn't like him."

"And that ruins his day? You can give him a message from me. Tell him I bleed for him."

"He bleeds for you," I said.

She shrugged.

"So what? Blood I don't need."

When we left her, I started back the way we had come, down toward the main corridor where the floor nurse had her station in the commanding position between the ward and the elevators. I was all the way down to the corridor before I noticed that the inspector wasn't with me. I trotted back. When I reached the door to Norah's little room, I could see just in passing that he hadn't returned to her. She was alone and climbing out of bed. I went on past her room, carrying on in the only direction Inspector Schmidt could have gone from there, continuing along the hall.

A few yards beyond Norah's door the hall took a right. After about twenty yards it took another right. There were other doors along the hall, but they were all shut and I could think of no reason for the inspector to have gone through any of them. I stayed with the hall. Around its second bend it ran straight, but there it came to a dead end at the glass-paneled doors to a ward. I caught up with the inspector there.

If I'd been thinking floor plan instead of dividing myself between thoughts of Norah Simms and speculation on what the inspector was up to, I wouldn't have had even a moment of disorientation. I followed the inspector down the central aisle of the ward. He was ignoring the beds lined up on both sides of the aisle, the patients in them, and the visitors grouped around them.

We were on our way out. At the far end of the ward the doors stood open. I could see into the corridor beyond. The desk was there and the nurse at her station. Beyond her desk were the elevators. She spotted us as soon as we came out of the ward. She rose and, standing by her desk, she waited for us. Promptly she was in there with the challenging question.

"Lose your way or did you sneak up on another patient without permission?"

"Just exploring," the inspector said.

"Exploring what?"

"The layout of your floor. Any place we go, we like to have a picture of all modes of access and all possible lines of retreat."

"You upset Norah and you thought you could sneak out without my seeing you?"

"Upset Norah?" The outrage of the suggestion shocked the inspector. "We left her laughing. We'd like to do the same for you."

"If you just leave, that'll be enough."

We left.

Coming out of the building, the inspector paused for a moment at the top of the front steps. He shot a quick look up and down the street before moving on. There didn't seem to be anything to look at, just the usual traffic, wheeled and pedestrian. Across the street in the shadowed recesses of a doorway something stirred. It was the doorway of a store that had been shut up for the night. A dim little spot of light brightened briefly and then whizzed in arcing flight from doorway to gutter. Someone standing back in the shadows over there had taken the final drag on a cigarette and then flicked away the glowing butt.

We came down the steps and started walking toward the corner. It was only a short way, a distance perhaps half as great as the width of the street. As we were about to turn the corner, we stopped and looked back. We were just in time to see the man as he took the hospital steps two at a time. It was a good guess that in the moments it had taken us to walk to the corner, the man who had flicked the cigarette had made it clear across the street. We had been walking. He would need to have done it on the run. It was only a quick glimpse we caught of him, but there was no possibility of mistake.

This was a man who had been with Norah Simms. The nurse had gone to haul him out of Norah's room and to tell him to make his exit the long way around through the ward. Returning to us and kicking her ethics in the face, she'd held us with her chatter till she could see that she could safely send us on to Norah without any possibility that we might find her patient not alone.

You know how nurses are about having too many visitors crowd a bedside all at once.

III.

We reached the station house a few minutes after the time Leary had set, but he was still tied up at his desk. We waited the better part of a half hour until he was through and then it was some minutes more while he changed out of his uniform. He was white-faced and spent. On him it looked terrible. This was a hard-bodied man, possessed of every kind of strength. A rock of a man, he wasn't built for wearing those looks of depletion and defeat. Seeing him was like watching a mountain crumble.

"Where do you want to eat?" he asked.

The question was for the inspector. There had been a time long in the past when he had been in this precinct. He might know the places. I didn't.

"It used to be there was no place but Dinah's," the inspector said.

"Still no place but Dinah's unless we go uptown, but Dinah's isn't like it used to be."

"She's still doing the soul food?"

"It's not the food. The food's never changed."

"So it's Dinah's."

We walked around to the restaurant. We would have walked right past it if Leary hadn't hauled the inspector back. Looking at it, the inspector shook his head.

"No," he said. "It can't be. Not the Dinah I knew. It wasn't in her to go cutesy."

Leary had warned him he would find the place changed.

He hadn't mentioned that the sign no longer said just "DI-NAH'S." What she had now ran the full length of the front. It needed all the space. She was calling the restaurant:

someone's in the kitchen with

DINAH

It seemed to be all red-checked gingham and red gera-niums.

"She had a decorator," Leary explained. "By the time she took her eye off the kitchen and came out for a look, it was too far along to change anything much and she wasn't about to put out the money for ripping it apart and starting over."

We went in and snagged a table. We were lucky to find one. It was the last not already taken. What Leary called the "carriage trade" was much in evidence. On a quick glance I spotted TV faces, movie faces, theater faces, music faces, gossip-column faces, and courtroom faces. You know the people who turn up on all the talk shows? Those shows could have been doing their casting by canvassing the tables at Dinah's. While the inspector hadn't been looking, it had become one of the "in" places.

Inspector Schmidt ran a hand over the red-checked tablecloth. He picked up a red-checked napkin and surveyed it with every evidence of suspicion.

"Tablecloths," he said. "Napkins. Upper-bracket big shots down here for upper-bracket slumming. She's run out on her old crowd."

"That'll be the day," Leary said. "We're here. Nobody's stopped coming. It's just that now she has these folks as well. They come from all over. So she's making a nice buck. Who deserves it more?"

"She used to get the people who wouldn't know what to

do with a tablecloth or a napkin. They're not coming in here."

"No. They go down the alley. There's another room. It's back of the kitchen and it's got an alley entrance. The decorator never got back there. Back there nothing's changed. It's just like Dinah's used to be."

The inspector started to push away from the table.

"Then what are we doing here?" he said. "Let's go down the alley."

"We wouldn't be welcome," Leary told him. "We'd embarrass people. She didn't do this big front to get rid of her old crowd. She set this up as a place where she could shunt the likes of us."

A waiter took our order. Leary gave him a message to carry to the kitchen. When Dinah had the time, she might want to come out and say hello to an old friend.

"Tell her it's a pain in the ass other people call Schmidt," the inspector added. "She'll remember better if you tell her it's the pain. For her I was never anything else."

Meanwhile I was wondering about that back room. I wasn't shocked. I wasn't of a mind to start any one-man crusade against it. There are back rooms all over town. If you think there aren't, you've been leading a sheltered life. Sometimes they are the scene for the neighborhood crap game. Sometimes they make book. Sometimes it's a clearing house for numbers runners or how about a massage parlor?

Whatever, they're against the law. The police know about them. They could move against them any time, but they don't move. I know you're beginning to mutter stuff about police corruption and what's to become of all the crap I fed you about what a supercop Schmitty is and what a great guy Wishes Leary is?

It's not that simple. Nothing ever is. It's the facts of life

and not only in our town. It goes for any city anywhere, I guess, and for a lot of places that aren't anywhere big enough to be called cities. What gives in all those back rooms is the small stuff. If all a department wanted was to build a great arrest record and the hell with law enforcement, the boys could move on every back room they know about and stuff the court calendars to capacity for all the rest of time. Then, when something big came along, they'd have no place to go to find all those little fellows who are the sources of the useful tips because they're the *quid pro quo* against the arrests that were never made and insurance against the arrests that could still be made.

If you don't know that much, I admire your innocence. Before you begin admiring mine, however, I'm going to tell you that I know the rest of it, too. It's not a great system. It's a stinkingly bad system, but a police department that didn't work on that system could hardly work at all. So you take the bad with the good and do what you can to hold the bad down and build up the good. Where you have a process that trades small immunities for large information, you hope you're not developing spots where small immunities will be traded for large cash payments.

Too often it's only a hope. I know that. We all know it. You can't work in law enforcement, or even just hang around a police department the way I do, without knowing it. I'm not going to say that the cash payments are corruption and that payment by information is not. Both are corrupt, but you have to draw the line between corruption practised for the public good and corruption practised for profit. It's a shabby compromise, but since we must live by it, we learn to live with it. For the police it's the choice between martyrdom and effectiveness. Martyrdom might

make them prettier in the eyes of the citizenry. Effectiveness makes them more useful to us, gives us, we hope, a less dangerous town to live in.

So I wasn't shocked. I can't say I wasn't curious. It's a matter of proportion. When you have a back-room racket that operates behind the screen of some legal business, it's most likely a small business out front and a much bigger operation behind the scenes. This front of Dinah's was no little business. Confronted with a screen of such dimensions and one that seemed to be doing so well, it staggered my imagination to try to conceive of the size of the thing Dinah might have had going in her back room.

I asked Leary about it.

He shook his head.

"Not like that," he told me. "Not with Dinah. No way. She's a one-woman Salvation Army, and she has been as long as we've known her. If you're hungry, you eat. If you can pay what it costs, okay. If you can't get up that much, it's pay what you can. If you can't pay at all, you still eat." He turned to the inspector. "You remember," he said.

Inspector Schmidt remembered.

"She always pretended it was yesterday's ribs, yesterday's chittlings, yesterday's sweet-potato pie because she couldn't serve the paying customers anything that hadn't been cooked fresh. So it was better someone ate it instead of throwing it out."

"Of course," Leary added, "there's never yesterday's anything because she's always fed yesterday's hungry mouths."

"But there never used to be a back room," the inspector insisted. "If you didn't like the company, you could go uptown to eat."

"Mostly in the back room they don't have table manners," Leary reminded him. "Some of them look dirty.

Hell, some of them are dirty. If she had them out here, they'd put the paying customers off. They'd be bad for business, and business has to stay good if she's going to go on being able to afford the handouts."

"And," I contributed, "once the place got to be the way it is now, the freeloaders would be shy of coming in. They wouldn't be comfortable with this crowd."

"The way it used to be," the inspector said, "there were some weren't comfortable with us then. A lot of them hung outside the door, and she passed stuff out to them. They ate in the street."

"Right," Leary said. "It had to be that way then because there was only the one room. Now that she has the two rooms, she can make it comfortable for everybody."

"So that's the whole of it?" I asked. "Dinner checks out front and food for free in the rear?"

"Neighborhood folks in the rear, whether they pay or not," Leary said. "Outsiders here."

"You're an outsider, Wishes? No more an old friend?"

"Old friend of Dinah's, Schmitty. At least I think—I guess—I hope. To the people she feeds back there I'm the pig you don't want on your plate. I'm *the* outsider."

"Your precinct, Wishes. How come it's wall-to-wall cop haters?"

Leary shrugged.

"The usual," he said. "We try to keep the station house clean. I won't pretend I can swear for every last one of my men. You know how that is. From one day to the next you can't be sure; but if there is anything going, we don't wink at it. It'll be only because we haven't found it."

What he was saying could account for the hostility of part of the neighborhood population. Gamblers, pushers, racketeers, and pimps prefer their police corruptible. For the officer they can bribe, they will work up a warm and

friendly feeling. To lose their love, he would have to be exorbitantly expensive and savagely grasping.

"The welfare mothers?" I asked. "What about them?"

"They get mugged. Their flats get hit by burglars. It happens all too often, but that's the same all over. Sometimes we get lucky and we fall into it right when it's happening. We make a collar, and it makes us friends."

The inspector looked sour.

"But not for long," he said. "It also raises expectations. They start asking why you don't hit it lucky every time, why you're not there for every mugging. Is it only because of questions like that you're losing friends?"

"Part of the reason," Leary said. "And we lose more than we gain. They come in with their complaints. We can't just let it go by without questioning them. Because we question them, they stop coming in. It ends up with us blamed for doing nothing about the ripoffs, including the ones we've never been told happened."

"Norah Simms," I said. "You did get the word on her."

Our food had come. Putting himself outside some of Dinah's cooking, Wishes Leary had begun to look better. Reminded of Norah, he put down his fork. He might have been losing his appetite.

"If they're hit so bad they need an ambulance," he said, "we always get the word. A Mothers' Day ripoff—that means she's lost the whole of her welfare payment, no money to go on with for two weeks. She puts in for emergency funds, and the word comes through to us from Welfare. It's the smaller hits that often go unreported. It'll be maybe a couple of bucks."

"And they won't see that without answers to your questions they leave you with your hands tied?" I asked.

Leary winced.

"Look," he said. "A kid's been hit bad. Her ribs are

cracked. She's miscarried. Is she going to like it when a cop gets to pushing her, trying to make certain she isn't faking it?"

"How do you fake broken ribs, not to speak of a miscarriage?"

"She's got the broken ribs," the inspector said, "and she's miscarried. Nobody's questioning that. But how did it happen? She says she was mugged. Could be she was. It could just as well be that she and the boyfriend got to fighting and he beat up on her, so why not cash in on it? She pushes the ripoff story. It gets her a duplication on the two-weeks' mother-of-dependent-children payment and emergency funds as well."

"She also has her pride," Leary added. "She doesn't let the other women or anyone else know that the guy she's shacked up with beats her."

"In a case like this one," the inspector said, "it's not too likely it's a game she and the boyfriend are playing together. A few bruises on a woman's throat—and they don't even have to be bad bruises—you put them together with a ripped dress and her hair mussed and it can be enough to set up the picture. Cracked ribs and miscarriage, though, they're extreme for that kind of caper."

"I'd say they were extreme for anything," I said.

"They are, they are," Leary said. "But when you've seen women with knife wounds or gunshot wounds or even dead and all at the hands of the loved one, you stop thinking there'll be any limits."

We kicked it around. Mothers of dependent children make up a major part of the public-assistance rolls. Some of them are widows. Others are unlucky types who've been married to guys who've run out on the wife and kids. Sometimes he's gone off with another woman. Sometimes he's only run out on his responsibilities. He can even be a

guy who's never been able to make enough to support his family and he figures that, without him and on welfare, they'll be better off. He's skipped for their sake.

Often enough she's an unmarried mother. She couldn't herself say which john fathered which kid and, even if she could, she wouldn't know where to find him. He's a married man. He has another family he's barely supporting or not supporting at all.

There you have a wide range of variations, but they don't cover the whole spectrum. Sometimes, married or not, the man has disappeared only for the welfare records. He has a flop somewhere and he keeps sufficiently out of sight for the woman to establish and maintain her eligibility for the mother-of-dependent-children benefits. He might have a job. Then between his earnings and their benefits they do a lot better than they could on his earnings alone.

He might also be a bum, and the benefits that are supposed to sustain her and the children are stretched to sustain him as well. They may also be spread impossibly thin if, in addition to everything else, they must maintain his drinking or his gambling or his drug habit.

It was this last situation that Leary had in mind. A woman who has escaped the attentions of the ripoff artists—and she is likely to escape their attentions if in the dark hallway she has waiting for her a strong-armed husband or a burly boyfriend—such a woman can work in collusion with her man to get some extra money out of the welfare people. Without roughing her up much, he puts on her such minimal marks as she might need to support a mugging story.

"On a woman with the kind of skin that bruises easily," the inspector said, "it doesn't have to be overemphatic."

"It has to be more than overemphatic before her ribs crack and she aborts," I said.

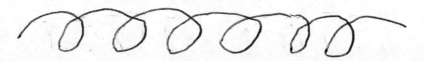

Neither Inspector Schmidt nor Captain Leary wanted to argue that. A woman who complains of having been mugged, backing up her story by showing minor bruises, might be a cooperative type who will rob her children so that she can keep some louse she's shacked up with.

The ones who turn up with more than minor marks, however, might still have received their injuries at the hands of the beloved. He wants more money than she's prepared to turn over to him. She gives him an argument. He beats up on her. Broken ribs might be the least of what he gives her.

"We get them like that," Leary said, "where that size beating is just too much. It's cured her of wanting him. Even then she'll maybe keep it to herself."

"Unless she's angry enough to turn him in," the inspector said, "or she has to turn him in because there's no other way to get rid of him."

"And Norah Simms?" I asked.

"You should see her kids," Leary said.

"We've seen them," the inspector told him. "Mallard had them with him."

"Then you know. You won't find brothers anywhere that are more look-alikes, and none of them look like her."

"They could be throwbacks to an earlier generation," I said. "Maybe they look like her father or her brother. It happens."

"One kid or two," Leary argued. "Sure it happens. But all of them?"

"So they all have the same father," the inspector said. "Obvious."

"Also obvious that she's never been without her man," Leary added. "They get together and regularly."

"Which also suggests that she shares the welfare money with him?" I asked.

"There's the pattern for it," the inspector said.

Leary shook his head.

"That there is, but only that much. For Norah Simms the rest of the pattern doesn't fit."

"Why not?" the inspector said.

"The way she is about the kids. She's a good mother and she's all mother. She could be crazy about a guy, but she'd kill him before she'd let him take a penny away from what she has for her boys. She's that kind of a woman. Her children are the main'event. A lot of these mothers—what they like is the good time. The kid is the price they pay for their fun. With Norah it's like the other way around."

"The guy is the price she pays for having still another baby?" I asked.

"And she sticks with him because he gives her such great babies," the inspector said.

"But no more," I reminded him.

"Unless she changes her mind."

We filled Leary in on the prattle we'd had from the hospital nurse.

"She'll change her mind," he said.

"As Dan Mallard would have told us long since," the inspector said, "it's her business and none of ours." He switched the subject to something that seemed more immediately germane. "According to Mallard," he said, "and we had it from Norah as well, that dump they live in has the neighborhood's top record for these muggings—often enough in the other buildings around but every last time in theirs."

Leary winced.

"Not quite every last time. It's such a regular thing there that I keep trying the obvious. I put a stakeout in the hall and then nobody turns up. It's every last time except when I have it staked out."

He didn't have to tell us that he couldn't stake out this one tenement building every time Mothers' Day came around. He had his whole precinct to cover and with limited manpower.

Dinah came out to say hello. She was nothing like I'd expected. I'd been picturing an Aunt Jemima type. Not jolly and smiling because I'd been warned that she would be dour, but on the rest of what they'd said of her, I'd been looking for a fat woman with a big, comfortable bosom.

She was big, but she wasn't fat. She was rawboned, spare, and severe. What there was about her kitchen smock that made it look more surgical than culinary, I don't know. It was probably just the air with which she wore it. Everything about her had the hard, practical, no-nonsense look. Her uncompromising gaze was in no way softened by her steel-rimmed spectacles. Her hair was mercilessly yanked back from her face and disciplined into a bun at the back of her head. The bun looked like a hard knot in a well-tarred rope. This was American Gothic in blackface.

She was affable enough, even though she didn't smile. She told me she was glad to meet me. She told Leary to relax because, the way he was going, he was working on an ulcer. When he got his ulcer made, he could stop coming around to her place.

"You'll be eating someplace else, Wishes," she said. "I don't go fussing with nobody's diets. If it's got to be I can't fry, it's going to be I don't cook."

Most of her attention, however, went to Inspector Schmidt. She didn't like the way he was looking. She remembered him as he had been back in his rookie days and she was telling him he hadn't changed enough. She looked at him and she looked at Leary.

"You and Wishes, you've got to be about the same age, Schmitty. I can remember when you were kids, breaking in

together, walking beat. Wishes doesn't look the way he did back then. He's aged like any decent man should. You? You still look like a boy. You're not aging at all. What's with you, Schmitty? Don't you ever care about anything? Don't you ever think about anything? Don't things ever worry you?"

"I've been out of the neighborhood," the inspector said. "I've had a carefree life. I've had you off my back."

She sniffed.

"It's time you had somebody on it. I bet you aren't married."

"Good bet."

"Why not? You want to be a kid all your life?"

If her looks had been unexpected, all the rest of this was even more so. If she came out at all, I'd thought it would have been just to say hello, a moment or two and then back to her kitchen. She had a place that wasn't going to run itself and, if there was anything about her that was obvious, it was that she ran the place. She wasn't a woman who would know how to delegate authority. She was a woman who wouldn't want to know, a woman who wouldn't ever let anything slide. I could have guessed that she had never in her life taken a vacation. I couldn't imaging her taking so much as a five-minute break.

So now she was taking five minutes or more. She let me pull up a chair for her. She sat with us. She had coffee and a wedge of her sweet-potato pie. She talked and she talked. If it had come from another woman, I would have called it chatter, a spate of small talk. This, however, was the woman who looked as though she never wasted anything, not even words. Even though she was sitting with us and wasting them in quantity, I had trouble believing my eyes and ears. The performance was too peculiar.

Our waiter put an end to it. Coming from the kitchen, he broke in on Dinah.

"It's done rising," he said. "You told me I should call you when it's done rising."

"All the way up to the top of the pan? Double what it was?"

She was pushing back from the table.

"All the way," the waiter said.

"Okay."

Dinah was on her feet. She had a quick glad-to-have-met-you for me. For Leary she had the suggestion that he go someplace and get drunk. For Inspector Schmidt she added to the advice she had been giving him.

"And you, Schmitty. You get yourself married. Don't take a lot of time looking for the right woman. The wrong one'll be okay too. The wrong one might do a quicker job on getting you caught up with your aging."

With that she left us. The waiter, however, stayed and handed us our check. Nobody had asked for it, and it's not good restaurant manners to give a customer a check before he's asked for it. Sometimes, when it's coming up closing time or your waiter is going off and he's afraid someone else will pocket his tip, the check might be pushed at you, but always with an apology and an explanation.

It was nowhere near closing time. The waiter had other tables where the people had finished their meal before us and were still lingering with cigars and cigarettes, and he hadn't pushed a check at any of them. I had to wonder why at us, unless Dinah wanted to rush us out of there so Leary could start getting drunk and Inspector Schmidt could begin looking for the wrong woman to marry. It still left her with no reason for wanting me to leave.

We paid the check and pulled out, but only as far as the

sidewalk out front. Inspector Schmidt was not yet ready to move on.

"Her back room?" he asked. "We get to it through the alley?"

Leary flipped his thumb in the direction of the dark opening along the restaurant's brightly lighted front.

"Just down there."

The ins   or started toward it.

"Let's drop back there and say good-by to Dinah," he suggested.

Leary dropped a hand on the inspector's arm.

"We haven't been invited," he said.

"An establishment open to the public?"

"More or less. For us it's rather less than more."

"So you know that, Wishes. There's no way Baggy and I could know. I'm curious. I want to see it."

"No way you could know it was there unless I told you, Schmitty."

"And she'll want to know why you didn't tell us it was off limits?"

Leary met question with question.

"How effective can I be if I am totally isolated in the district, if I have no friends around here at all. They're already too few. I can't risk losing even one more, not just for idle curiosity, even if it's your curiosity, Schmitty."

"You know better than that," the inspector said. "In our line of work curiosity is never idle."

"Okay. What do you expect to see back there?"

"If I knew, I maybe wouldn't need to go back and look. Tell me, Wishes. Did it ever happen before that Dinah came out front and sat down with you, not to speak of that much time?"

"I'm always around. It's been a dog's age since she'd

seen you last. She didn't sit down with me, Schmitty. She sat down with you. She's fond of you, Inspector."

"Flattery will get you et cetera, et cetera. I have another question, Captain. Has it ever happened before that one of her waiters pushed your check at you before you asked for it?"

"You think that was on Dinah's orders?"

"How much happens in there that isn't?"

Captain Leary did some thinking. He did it aloud.

"She sat with us and talked all that garbage about ulcers and wives and looking your age. She fed us all that crap so she could keep us pinned down out front until she got the word that the time had come when she would want us moved on."

"And when the time came, she wanted us moved and quick, Wishes. Any other way to spell it?"

Leary didn't try to suggest another way. He started for the alley. This time it was Inspector Schmidt dropping a hand on his old friend's arm.

"You don't have to go," he said. "You don't have to say any more good-by since you see her all the time. If she's going to get mad, let her get mad at me."

Leary wasn't having it.

"No good, Inspector. If she gets mad at you, it'll rub off on me anyhow. More than that, if there's anything on, how come I walk away from it? It is my precinct."

So Captain Leary led the way. Seen from the street, where the light along the restaurant's front was all but day-light-bright, the dark of the alley entrance looked the blackest of black. Once we had turned into the darkness, however, it took only a couple of steps before we realized that the black was not nearly that total. There were windows along the alley and light was coming through some of them. They would be Dinah's kitchen windows, easily

identifiable by the cooking fragrances that came wafting out of them. Between one bank of windows and the next, we could make out the darker recess of a door. It was easy enough to read that for the entrance to the kitchen, and the similar recess beyond the second bank of windows would be the entrance to the restaurant's back room. Less easy to read, as we came down the alley, was the huddled shape that lay on the pavement against the wall, just a few steps short of that last door.

It could have been a heap of rags. It could have been a starving man who, on his way to Dinah's for a handout, had not quite made it. He had fallen in a faint or, on the very threshold of the feast, had even starved to death. It could have been a wino sleeping off his muscatel or a head fallen into a heroin stupor.

But it was none of these. As soon as we'd spotted it, Inspector Schmidt hurried down the alley to it. Captain Leary and I were at his heels. Leary broke out his flashlight. Only in part was it a heap of rags. The rags were blood-soaked and in them was the body of a man. The man was dead. He had been long enough dead for the body to have gone cold but not so long that it was showing even the first signs of the onset of rigor.

From the way the body looked, it seemed evident that we weren't going to have to wait for any autopsy report to know the way of his dying. There was a spectacular bruise along the line of his jaw, but even with the swelling there was a crumpled look. Under the contusion there had to be a fractured jawbone. That, however, was the minor damage. The major injury was to the back of the man's head. It might even be said that there was no back to the man's head. It had been battered to a pulpy nothing.

So now everything had changed. Now it was murder. Inspector Schmidt, Chief of Homicide, was automatically in charge.

The body was lying on its right side, the face half turned down toward the pavement. The way he lay, the battered mess was faced right up at us. The rags he wore were tattered jeans and a torn T-shirt. Behind the left shoulder, the one on which the body was not lying, there was a large rent in the grimy fabric of the shirt. The skin of the man's back showed through the rent, and it exhibited a blue cast in contrast to other exposed areas of the body where the skin, if it wasn't blood-smeared or discolored by contusion, displayed the yellow-tinged gray that is the color of death.

To the inspector, no less than to me, there was nothing about the corpse that was recognizable, even though just about everything about it was all too familiar. It was not the body of anyone we knew, but in the course of time in Homicide, Inspector Schmidt had seen at least a thousand of him; and in my time with the inspector, I'd seen my share.

Medium height and medium weight, he had perhaps been exceptionally heavy of muscle for a man of his size; but to have noticed that, one would need to have looked at him with close interest or better still to have tangled with him hand to hand. From those limited areas where his hair was not bloodstained, you could know its color, and that was like the rest of him, neither one thing nor the other. Medium long, medium dark, it was unmemorable.

When I said the inspector and I had seen our many of him, I was thinking of at least a thousand criminal nondescripts. Pickpockets and cutpurses have the look as do sneak thieves and smash-and-grab operators.

So that was it. To the inspector and me the dead man didn't look like anyone we'd seen. He merely looked like

virtually all the smash-and-grab suspects there had ever been.

Wishes Leary, however, had an immediate make on him.

"Eddie Blue," he said. "Mostly people called him Black and Blue. He never got anywhere in the ring and it's been years since he was even trying. He was more than strong enough but he was always too stupid. As a fighter he was punchy before he ever took his first punch."

Leary had known him well, even to an exasperating degree. To hear him tell it, this Eddie Blue had long been a major item in his catalogue of frustrations.

"As far as I know, even back when he was getting fights —and that was way back and it wasn't for long—he never pulled down anything but the loser's end of a purse and you know how that is. You have to mix the losses up with a decent number of wins if you're going to put any fat on what you get at the loser's end. It's a cinch he didn't build himself any nest egg out of what he won in the ring."

"And no visible means of support ever since?"

"None. That's it. None, not ever. I don't think there's been anyone we've brought in more often without even once being able to make anything stick."

If you're a policeman, it's a thing you must learn to live with—this disconcerting spread between your own certainties and what before a judge and jury can be made to stand up as established fact. The Eddie Blues, with their peculiar gift for looking never so much like their individual selves as they resemble their general type, again and again, through the failure of any witness to come up with a solid identification, escape the consequences of their criminal acts.

"Is this the man?" you ask.

"He could be," the witness answers. "He looks like the man."

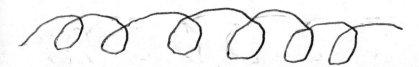

And that's it. "Could be" and "looks like" aren't nearly enough for knocking over the presumption of innocence.

Captain Leary stayed with the body. When we left him, he was whistling down a passing squad car to bring in his precinct detectives. They would be taking over the routine aspects of the investigation. The inspector and I pressed on through the alley. Any question of whether or not we would be welcome in Dinah's back room had now assumed a new dimension. Actually we were welcome in the back room and even in the kitchen. It might have been because it was lonely back there. It was empty—no customers and no free loaders, nobody but Dinah herself and the people she had working for her.

The floor of the back room had been freshly scrubbed. Its vinyl tiles still showed wet spots. The oilcloth table coverings also showed wet spots. They too had been freshly scrubbed. No table stood uncleared and whatever dishes or cutlery might have been used back there that night had been tossed into the giant dishwasher where great whooshes of hot water were even then sloshing everything clean.

Get the picture? It's a restaurant. Dishes are being washed. Can you call the dishwashing into question, even if you are assailed by the suspicion that it has all been a quick and efficient operation designed for the destruction of evidence? Obviously you couldn't but, no less obviously, Inspector Schmidt would try to find a way.

"Salt cellars," he muttered, making it sound as though he were trying to remember. "Pepper shakers, ketchup bottles, mustard pots, and sugar bowls—I remember those on every table."

Calmly Dinah added an item that had slipped the inspector's mind.

"Also Worcestershire sauce," she said.

"Even if you are making them take it as it comes, seasoned only the way you serve it, don't you have to allow them sugar for their coffee?"

Dinah grinned.

"Sugar for their coffee and all the rest of it, too, but always in clean sugar bowls, in clean bottles, in clean shakers. Nobody ever picks anything up and feels the dry crustiness of yesterday's drips. It can spoil a body's appetite."

"And when it isn't dry but still gummy, it might take beautiful fingerprints."

Dinah shrugged.

"Me," she said. "I feed people. I don't take their fingerprints. If you're wanting fingerprints, you're in the wrong place."

"Forget the prints, Dinah. I'm sorry, but you know from way back I'm a pain in the ass. We're in the right place."

"That means something?"

"It means that in your alley, right outside your door, there's a dead body. It used to belong to a guy named Eddie Blue. You may have known him as Black and Blue. He's dead and there's a lot of blood on him. The way the body looks, somebody knocked him cold and then finished him off by battering his head in. After all that—this is also the way the body looks—he was moved."

Dinah scowled.

"For me then he wasn't moved nearly far enough. I'd like him moved clean away from my place. Is that too much to ask?"

"In good time," the inspector said, "the body will be moved to the morgue. We always do that, you know."

"I know," Dinah said, "but maybe not quick enough. A thing like that for people to step over if they want to come in and eat, it'll turn anybody off. I couldn't figure it, but

now I know. It's always jumping back here and now look at it. It's like somebody up and abolished getting hungry."

"Like that?" the inspector asked. "Or like I'm thinking?"

Dinah cocked an eyebrow at him. There was heavy sarcasm coming.

"Like you're thinking. You're thinking whoever it was knocked off that Blue bastard came straight on in and slapped his fingerprints on all the sugar bowls and ketchup bottles."

"You know we can do better than that," the inspector said.

"I know nothing. You tell me."

"He was knocked cold and then his head was knocked in. After he was dead, his body was moved. If it was done in here and the body tossed out to the alley, there would be blood that needed scrubbing up."

"I wouldn't take the trouble. I'd tell you it was only ketchup."

"He wasn't in here tonight?"

"He's never in here. I don't serve just anybody."

"All right. Not just anybody. So who was here tonight?"

"Nobody. Who would come through the alley when that disgusting thing was lying out there and they'd have to step over it?"

"You saw the body?"

"Saw it? Are you crazy, man? I'd see it and just leave it there to rot? If I'd seen it, I'd have been yelling for the police. They couldn't have gotten it away from there fast enough to suit me and that still goes. I want it away from my place."

"Since you didn't see it, how do you know it's disgusting? Who told you?"

"You did. You said he's out there with his head bashed

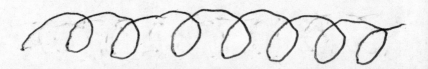

in and all over bloody. Without any of that he was disgusting, so the way you say he is . . . "

Even though nobody could believe a word of it, Dinah was on unassailable ground. The inspector was doing himself no good talking to her. We went back out to the alley. The technicians had taken over out there and, although they had just about finished their work on the body and on the alley, they had nothing for the inspector that hadn't been obvious after the first cursory examination of the corpse and of the place where it lay.

It was only when they picked the body up to haul it away that anything further turned up. Torn and soiled and blood-smeared, it had been lying under the body. It was in bad shape, but not so bad that it wasn't easily readable. It was an identity card. The name on it was Norah Simms, the address was as we'd had it from Dan Mallard.

Inspector Schmidt looked at his watch.

"Even if she's still in the hospital," he said, "just trying to talk to her this time of night would be put down as harassment."

The statement was indisputable, but it seemed to me that it rested on premises that were too wild even for the leaping Schmidt intuitions.

"Even if," I said. "Of course, she's still in the hospital. They don't let them out to hemorrhage in the street."

"Patients don't always wait around for formal discharge."

"That floor nurse—who walks out past that dragon?"

"Norah Simms knows that maternity ward. It's been her second home. If there's a way of sneaking out, she'd know it."

"And she ups from her bed of pain to swing on a professional fighter, not to speak of breaking the man's jaw with one mighty punch." The inspector started to answer me on

that, but I wasn't letting him in with it. I talked right on. "I know. I know," I said. "He was only an ex-fighter and even in his heyday he never had a heyday. At his best he was a stumblebum, and we have Mallard's word for it that she's a fighter. I know all that, but it doesn't make her big and powerful. Even if she were well, she wouldn't be up to it."

"She has friends with the necessary size and muscle," the inspector reminded me. "Mallard for one and possibly Dinah."

"You get mugged," I said. "Along with the money loss, you have the nuisance losses—driver's license, credit cards."

"Welfare mothers aren't likely to have credit cards."

"So it's just an identification card. It's something she carried in her purse. Her purse is snatched. The card is gone with everything else."

"Right. The mugger keeps the money. That isn't identifiable. He rids himself of the purse and all identifiable papers. It doesn't have to be a credit card. It's something with her name on it."

"Obviously, Schmitty. So what sends you off on this speculation about whether she's still in the hospital?"

"The story, Baggy. The story as we had it from Mallard and again as we had it from her. It's a story that fits the way things are in these parts. Even in safer neighborhoods a lot of women have quit carrying purses. Too much purse snatching going on. Around here nobody carries a purse, and she didn't. She had the money tucked down in her bosom."

I picked it up.

"And she had the identity card down there with the money. The mugger reached in and hauled out the whole wad. It makes sense."

"That's okay," the inspector said. "All the same I have a

gut feeling. I'm wondering about the cover-up Dinah is working on. I'm making guesses on the people Dinah would cover up for."

"On the basis of the card, you're assuming that Blue was the lug who ripped her off?"

"Blue may have been the man or Blue may have been framed," the inspector said. "It doesn't matter. Dinah believes he was the guy who hit Norah, and she thinks he got no more than he had coming to him. She's gone all out to cover the tracks of whoever it was she thinks gave Blue what he had coming to him."

"Right, Schmitty. Dinah can be thinking all of that, and she can be thinking it just as well with Norah Simms nicely tucked up in the hospital. The two things don't connect."

"Someone was in Dinah's back room this evening. This was somebody I'm not to know about because, Baggy, this will be someone who'd leap to the eye as the most natural suspect."

"Norah Simms doesn't leap to my eye," I said.

"If she hasn't left the hospital, she can't leap to anyone's eye. That much I can pin down."

We went around to the hospital, but the inspector pinned nothing down. He asked how Norah Simms was doing. They hoped she was doing all right. They didn't know. She wasn't up in the maternity ward anymore. She had been there when the evening visiting hours began. When they were over, she was gone. She had sneaked out. The inspector went into exact times. She had been up and away in what seemed to have been only minutes after we'd left her.

It was another one for the Schmidt intuition. Just taken by itself it was impressive, but can you see that it could have been getting him anywhere?

IV.

We headed back to the precinct station house. When he went out to dinner with us, Leary had been calling it a day; but murder changes everything. Wishes Leary cannot sleep on murder. He knew everything we knew—the identification card, Norah's unsanctioned pull-out from the hospital, the scrub-up of Dinah's back room, and the story that Dinah and her people were putting out. Nobody had eaten there that evening. Nobody had so much as come near the back room. He even had for the inspector an additional bit Schmitty hadn't picked up.

"The boys have checked Norah out," he reported. "She went home to her kids. Dan Mallard is great with them and all that, but he isn't their mother."

"He isn't anybody's mother," I said.

"Anyhow," Leary said, "that's her story. Her boys needed her and she didn't need the hospital. Anything they could do for her she could do for herself. She wanted to be with her kids."

"It's not unreasonable," I said. "Fresh from losing a baby, she could very well have come down with a hysterical need for being with the ones she had. It's a switch mothers pull all the time. They tell themselves their kids need them, when the truth of it is they need their kids."

"She been told about Blue?" the inspector asked.

"She's been told," Leary said. "She isn't interested. She told the boys she has her own troubles."

"And her identity card?"

"She's confused about that."

Leary fed us the full rundown on what his detectives had had from Norah. At first she refused to believe that the card had been turned up under the dead man's body. She had reacted with nothing but suspicion. She didn't know what sort of a phony the detectives were trying to pull, but would they please go away and not bother her with it? She had the card. It was stupid to try to make her believe they'd found it. She showed them the drawer where she said she kept it; and the boys reported that she put on a terrific act of being completely certain that all she needed to do was open it up and she'd have them confounded.

Not satisfied with that, the detectives insisted on seeing the card. She opened the drawer. She looked for the card. She appeared to be shocked at not finding it. She upended the drawer over her kitchen table, spilling everything out of it and searching for the card.

Of course, it wasn't there, but even then she'd refused to concede anything. She all but crawled inside the emptied drawer, searching it as though she thought the card had tucked in somewhere and was hiding from her and that, if she looked hard enough, she would somehow root it out. Having gone on with the futile search as long as she could, she'd then given up on the whole thing. She didn't understand it, but she was too tired and too sick to try to understand it. Anyhow it didn't matter. If they would just go away, she could lie down and get herself some rest.

"Not to speak of the time she might need for dreaming up a better story," the inspector said.

Leary shrugged.

"I don't know, Schmitty," he said. "The kid's been through a lot. She's had a rough day. Who's to say she isn't honestly confused?"

"Not me, Wishes. It's the logical, neatly patterned stories you want to suspect. That's the kind that's most likely

invented. For most people, the stuff of life comes mixed up and confused."

"Particularly," I said, "for a person who's fresh from the hospital and from the kind of day she's had. Every variety of emotional beating and that doesn't help a woman to make sense. Also it's a good bet that they had her full of sedation, and we know how that works."

Inspector Schmidt knew.

"It's supposed to knock you on your ass and give you some sleep when you need it most. But if your trouble is anxiety and the anxiety is strong enough, nothing knocks you out. You stumble around all fuzzed up with it."

"Which is the way she is tonight," Leary told him.

"Right," the inspector said, "and she's smart enough to know it and smart enough to avoid risking any answers till she's got her head clearer and she can think up a good one. You know that, Wishes."

Leary had to agree but he didn't have to like it.

"I know, Schmitty, I know," he said. "But I know something else, too. Work at it hard enough and you get to the place where you can't ever believe anybody or anything."

"And you know," the inspector told him, "that's close to the place where a good detective has to keep himself. You can't believe anybody. With anything, it's different. You can believe a corpse with a bashed-in jaw and a broken head. You can believe a restaurant dining room that long before closing time has been put through a spring-cleaning type scrub-up. You've got to believe that, but you can't believe it just happened that nobody ate in there tonight and that, only for that reason, Dinah grabbed the opportunity to do what amounts to a complete renovation. You have to keep that part of it open. The odds ride on its going the other way. Just because certain people did eat in Dinah's back room tonight, Dinah felt compelled to scour everything anyone might have touched."

There was no arguing that part of it. Even I had been thinking about the way Dinah had dismissed the inspector's suggestion of the possibility of fingerprint elimination.

"She knows nothing about fingerprints," I said. "That's another way of saying she knows a lot about them and all of it wrong. They were scrubbing away at stuff that could never have taken a print."

"Right," the inspector said. "Not knowing what might need doing, she had everything done, except that there may also have been blood spatterings to wash away."

"Not all over that big room and not on every last thing in the place," I said.

"Let's not underestimate Dinah. We see a place that gives every evidence of having been spot-washed, Baggy. I ask what was washed off the spot. Dinah's a brain. She wouldn't pinpoint it for me."

By the time Inspector Schmidt left off kicking around the possibilities with Captain Leary, we were well into the night. Leary wasn't going home. He had one of those leather sofas in his office. It was lumpy, but it had been on nights like this that it had developed the lumps and maybe they conformed not too badly to the Leary body. He could catch some sleep on it and still be there for anything that might break. It couldn't have been that murder was such a rarity in his precinct that it would demand of him such a vigil. Obviously it was a murder that might involve Norah Simms that made the demand.

The inspector and I pulled out. I was ready to call it a night. The inspector was not.

"I'm going visiting," he said.

I looked at my watch. Midnight had been and gone. We'd had a long day, and so had everyone else. This was going to be inhuman.

"At this hour?"

"The best time for catching people at home."

"Do you need to catch anyone right now? Can't you let her sleep?"

"Dan Mallard has a healthy rib cage and he hasn't miscarried. He called on us. Isn't it good manners to return a call?"

"Because he made noises about not calling it murder?"

"That and because he can tell us when and where Norah Simms took the troops off his hands."

"If he will."

"If he will, and if he won't that will be interesting, too. I'm curious."

"You're always curious."

"And you're always sleepy, or at least one hell of a lot of the time."

"This late I'm always sleepy. What's wrong with that?"

"Nothing. You go home to bed. I'll fill you in tomorrow."

I've had that from him before. It's an empty gesture. The inspector does it to lift the weight of my heavy eyelids off his conscience. He knows I'll never take him up on it. I didn't.

The tenement, taken just for itself and apart from its tenants, offered no surprises. It seemed typical, neither worse than most nor appreciably better. The halls weren't totally dark, but they were as poorly lit as Norah Simms had indicated. We saw neither the rats nor the roaches, but then more adequate lighting might have revealed them.

Mallard had told us that he occupied one of the rears, but he hadn't specified the floor. In the building vestibule there were the usual bell buttons and letter boxes. Where the boxes still had doors, however, the doors hung open. Nobody had bothered to label them with tenants' names. The bells looked as though they could never have been rung within the memory of even the oldest living occupant. They sat in rusty sockets, and the rust held them sealed in

place. Like the letter boxes, they were unlabeled. Nobody had bothered.

The inspector headed for the ground-floor rear. Pressing his ear against the door panel, he listened. I tried my own ear at it. It was about as thin as a door can be, but there wasn't even the first whisper of sound coming through it.

"Do you think you'll hear him flex the muscles?" I asked.

If I had been hearing even the smallest sound through the door, I would have thought to hold my voice down to a whisper. From the silence, however, I was assuming either emptiness beyond or tenants sound asleep. I spoke in ordinary tones. That doesn't mean I shouted. I was just average audible.

The inspector wasn't. When he came back to me, it was only in a whisper.

"Flimsy doors. Any talk or movement inside we'll hear. We're not going through the building waking people up just to ask which door."

Taking my cue from him, I also dropped to a whisper.

"I was afraid we were about to do just that."

"And make enemies when we don't have to?"

"Barging in on people this time of night you expect to make friends?"

"Dan Mallard's an antiestablishment type. With him disregard of middle-class conventions could build up a fellow feeling."

I was about to tell the inspector not to count on it, but I never got to say it. We were leaning against the door. Abruptly it was jerked out from under us. Everything came down on us at once. Light stabbed our eyes, and some sort of missile whizzed at our heads. That the thing was wielded with lethal intent seemed obvious, but our assailant had miscalculated. Too much of our weight had been propped against the door. When the door was jerked away from us, the two of us went off balance and toppled forward. The thing cut a whistling slice out of the air precisely at the level where our heads would have been had we been caught while standing upright. As we were, it passed above our heads. Only by the smallest margin, however, did it miss giving us a pair of flattop haircuts.

My first thought was ridiculous. It was that the thing being swung at us had to be a mace or a flail or some such contrivance of medieval weaponry. You know, it's the great, heavy hunk of iron swung at the end of a chain and guaranteed to pulp anything it meets.

I wasn't stopping to examine it. I just kept going the way my momentum had started me. It rammed me into our assailant. I made contact at gut level. Since I was in no position for seeing much of anything, I didn't see him do it; but from the results I know that Inspector Schmidt went for the weapon. When we untangled, he came up with the thing in his hand. I came up with its owner. I also came up with a clawed cheek, a bitten finger, and a pair of shins with some notches kicked into them.

My opponent was neither large nor heavily muscled. However, whatever might have been lacking in weight and strength was compensated by speed and ferocity. There was never any question of how we would come out. Once that first wild swing had missed us, we had to end up on top. That initial onslaught had been the all-or-nothing shot. All the rest was desperation, but there was enough desperation to keep it from being any easy win for our side.

Eventually, though, the inspector had the weapon, and I had our assailant pinned to the floor. I looked at the inspector's prize, and he looked at mine. His was a rusted electric iron made nastily spiky by the attached shards of its broken handle. That it had been carefully prepared for

weapon use was obvious. Its cord had been doubled over to make a loop handle of convenient swinging length, and the remainder of the cord had been wrapped around the body of the iron and well secured.

Bemused with the thought of the damage that iron could have done if it had met flesh and bone, I forgot for the moment about getting myself and my adversary up off the floor. The inspector reminded me.

"Manners, Baggy," he said. "Manners. Isn't it time you helped the lady up?"

This must sound dim. Any fool, no matter how wild the fight, would certainly have picked up on the innumerable anatomical indications of the fact that he was tangled with a female. I can only say I had been giving no thought to what I was tangled with. If asked, I might very likely have said a wildcat. I looked at her and found myself further justification. She was not only a woman. She was an old woman, old enough to have suffered considerable shrinkage in those parts that most arrestingly identify the female, so much shrunken, in fact, that you would expect that she might have been considerably enfeebled as well, but that she wasn't.

I adjusted my grip to something more polite, but I was careful to relinquish nothing of control.

"If I let you up," I asked her, "can I trust you to be a lady?"

"You can trust me to claw your eyes out."

I kept my hold on her.

"Why?" the inspector asked.

"Creeping up on my door. Hanging there right outside and as bold as brass. This time of night what are you going to be here for? Not to fix the plumbing. Raping and robbing. All right. It happens to some. It don't happen to me. Not without a fight, it don't."

"We're looking for one of your neighbors," the inspector said.

His tone couldn't have been milder, but the lady was not mollified.

"Go try someplace else. This house has had its trouble for today."

The inspector looked at his watch.

"Past midnight," he said. "That was yesterday."

The lady had begun to simmer down, not enough to induce me to risk turning her loose but sufficiently to suck me in. I relaxed a bit. I couldn't see where the inspector's words could warrant a resumption of violence. They had that effect.

Spitting and cursing, she flailed around in my grip, but this time less effectively. It wasn't that she was trying any the less. In the way of the aged, she could be up to mustering her strength for the one shattering outburst, but it would have to be the all-or-nothing shot. Win or lose, it wouldn't leave her much. Second effort is for the young. What little she could come up with, furthermore, was being expended on shouted curses and on spitting.

If her first assault on us had been self-defense, an effort to forestall what she had assumed would be an attack, this new outburst seemed to be born of nothing more than reluctance to admit that her initial reaction to us had been mistaken. She had to be past any delusion of taking effective action against us.

"Dan Mallard," the inspector said. "He's a big guy. He's got the size for taking care of himself."

She stopped short, but it was only the anger that went out of her. Suspicion remained.

"Danny Boy? What would you be wanting with Danny Boy?"

"Talk, just talk."

She opened up a gap-toothed grin. She chuckled. I took the chance that the grin and the chuckle might mean peace had broken out. Letting go of her, I offered a hand to help her to her feet. She gave the hand a look of malevolence. Scrambling up off the floor, she did it on her own. The effort took all her breath. Once upright, however, she made a quick recovery.

"Talk," she said. "You're going to the right one for that. That Danny, he's a talker. He'll talk the ear off of a teacup."

"He said a rear apartment. He forgot to say which floor."

For that, the grin and the chuckle didn't suffice her. She laughed. It was a bark of bitter mockery.

"An apartment is it? It's a hole the like of this one."

"Up how many?" the inspector asked.

"Up yours," the lady said.

The inspector stepped back into the hall.

"Thanks for everything," he said.

I followed him out.

"It's been nice meeting you," I said.

She slammed the door after us. Inspector Schmidt was already on the stairs. I started up after him.

"With all that cooperation," I asked, "now what?"

"Mallard will be the next one up."

The inspector couldn't have sounded more certain.

"If she told us," I said, "it went past me."

"She was making like Mallard's butler, announcing his guests. Just enough uproar nicely calculated to alert him to get set for us."

"We still don't know what floor."

"One flight. If she'd needed to make her warning carry more than one flight, she would have been noisier."

The reasoning was all right, but I thought it rested on too many unverifiable assumptions. I never got to say so

since by then we were up that first flight, and Dan Mallard was there, leaning in his doorway, waiting for us. He was unarmed and he was assuming no postures, whether defensive or belligerent. He was relaxed and looked mildly amused, smiling inwardly at some private joke. He didn't keep it private. Without waiting even for a greeting, he shared it with us.

"I told Dinah it wasn't going to work," he said. "If you know Dinah, though, she's got the delusion that nothing is beyond her. Actually so very little is that it mostly makes no difference. 'Nothing ventured, nothing gained,' she said. Now there's a cliché that could run closer to the truth to save people a lot of grief. 'Nothing ventured, nothing lost' would be better."

"You ate there tonight?"

"I had a lot of mouths to feed including my own big mouth, so where else? Anyhow, I never eat anywhere else, not if I can help it. My career depends on that most muscle-building fodder Dinah cooks."

"Back room?"

"Always. The front's as bad as uptown."

"Through the alley?"

"On the way in. Through the front room on the way out because there was blood and mashed brain out in the alley, and people worry about letting the little ones see that sort of stuff. They think it'll traumatize the infant minds. I told her not to worry. The kids would enjoy it. She thought she knew better."

"Suppose we take this inside," the inspector said, "or do you have company?"

"Not until you come in." Mallard shaped up some over-elaborate gestures of welcome. "Beer or cocoa," he said. "You name it, and no need to feel indebted. It's canned beer and instant cocoa. I get both for free—sponsors' products. The muscles sell them."

V.

The muscles might have sold the beer and the cocoa, but the rest of him was out to sell an appearance of guileless innocence. He was not a man who'd run when none pursued. More than that, even if there were pursuit, Dan Mallard would never deign to run.

"You saw the body?" the inspector asked.

"I went out and looked—a cheap thrill and for free even. Why should I pass it up?"

"Know the man?"

"Used to see him around. He was never any buddy of mine."

"But you knew who he was?"

"A rat. The exterminator doesn't always miss."

"The exterminator? You know who?"

Mallard went into a one-man dialogue, shooting questions and capping them with his own quick anwers.

"The extermination of rats is done by exterminators. Right? Right. 'It follows as the night the day.' "

By my visceral clock it was long past the hour for nonsense. I was wondering how much of this stuff the inspector might feel compelled to take.

"Now it's Shakespearean muscle," I said.

"Clichésville, brother," Mallard said. "Within every clown lurks the yen to play Hamlet. Within this clown it's Polonius."

"Why not some plain talk?" the inspector said, though it was evident that he wasn't expecting any.

"Like what?"

"Like how did you know he was a rat?"

"By his long, naked tail. He looked like a rat. Now he's had a rat's end, and I don't mean his tail."

"Just how much did you know about him?"

"Enough so I saw him where he lay and I never dropped a tear."

"Let's try taking this from the top," the inspector said.

"Up, down, or sideways, you'll get no tears."

"Tears we don't need."

"What do you need?"

"Information. Straight answers."

"Easy," Mallard said. "Their mom was in hospital and I had to see to feeding the troops. I wouldn't make those poor, defenseless little hellions eat my cooking. Hell! I don't eat it myself. Since for me the answer is Dinah's, it was the answer for them as well. They eat early. I mean they get hungry early. In this part of town kids don't eat every time they get hungry; although with the mom they've got, they do better than most."

The route he was going, the night could have been too short for him to come around to anything material.

"Sociological background we can fill in for ourselves," the inspector said. "Suppose we move along to murder."

"Extermination."

It was so dispassionate. He might have been giving the inspector a language lesson.

"The rat was human."

The inspector can give language lessons, too.

"Was he now? I could argue that."

"And you probably will. Your neighbor downstairs said you could talk the ear off a teacup."

"That old biddy! Probably the nicest thing she ever said about me. Maybe even the nicest thing she ever said about

anyone. Most of what comes out of her mouth is unrepeatable."

"And loud enough to tip you to visitors before anyone has time to climb the stairs."

Mallard laughed.

"That," he said, "would be what you might prefer to recognizing her words for what they were—her considered opinion of you."

"Back to the kids and their getting hungry early. It was there you began to wander."

"No wandering at all. I took them to Dinah's, Dinah's back room, by the shortest route."

"Through the alley and no corpse to fall over?"

"No garbage of any description. You should know Dinah. She keeps an immaculately tidy alley."

"I know Dinah."

"I fed well and the kids fed well," Mallard said. "At Dinah's you never eat less than well, but tonight—for me up to my ears in good deeds and the kids up to their ears in disaster—quite naturally she outdid herself. Never a biscuit rose to such heights. Never did pig's ears more succulently grace the black-eyed peas, never . . . "

The inspector snatched the never right out of the big lug's mouth.

"Never mind the rest of your nevers. You ate and, while you were eating, somebody messed up that immaculate alley with a small act of murder."

"Exactly."

"You were busy eating. Dinah was busy cooking. You were inside. It was outside. How did you get the word?"

"We were told. You know how people are. They will talk. In Dinah's back room people talk all the time. Even with their mouths full, they talk."

"Someone came in from the alley," the inspector

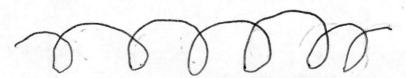

prompted. "He came in and said: 'Guess what. There's a fresh-killed stiff lying across the doorstep. I had to step over it to get in.'"

"Maybe not those exact words," Mallard said, doing the big bit on being scrupulously exact in the information he was giving us. "Something like that. You've come close. It was words to that effect."

"And who was it who came in and spoke words to that effect?"

"Now you're asking too much. That I don't remember."

"Try."

"No use. I'll never remember."

"What do you remember?"

"I remember what I ate. I remember what the kids ate. I remember going out to the alley to look at it. I didn't think it could be as bad to look at as reported, and I was sure I could herd the troops past it to take them home. So I looked at it, and it was as I'd thought, but Dinah didn't agree. I had to wait and take the kids out the front way. She wasn't going to risk having their little psyches damaged for life. I remember waiting. I remember being busier than a bird dog holding the little ones back from putting their grubby little fingers on anything that had already been scrubbed clean because Dinah had the notion that you guys might even be dumb enough to think the baby, risen up in his diaper, could have bashed that guy's head in with a teething ring. I remember getting the all-clear and marching the troops out past the quality in Dinah's front room. I remember taking them home and turning them over to their mom, and that's about all the remembering this poor head can handle."

"You and the kids weren't the only ones eating there tonight."

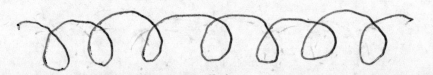

"Not by a long shot. In the front room she was doing capacity."

"The back room?"

"In the back room I was eating and, when I eat, I can't see past my plate. Passing through the front room, I had finished eating. I was up to noticing things."

So that was the pattern of the remembering he would profess, and there was no way to move him off it. He was the eager witness. He would try to compensate for all he wanted the inspector to believe he couldn't remember by recounting, with the greatest superfluity of detail, those things he chose to remember. He was, of course, not admitting that he was making such a choice, but the boundaries of his memory were too neatly exact to have been set by anything but calculation.

Having never had any faith in Dinah's strategem, he was making no effort to pretend that he had not witnessed the big scrub-up or that he remembered nothing of it. Similarly, whether out of a conviction that he was beyond suspicion or because he would not stoop to lying in his own interest or in the belief that he could volunteer enough to make the inspector think that, so far as his own possible involvement might have gone, he'd told us all, he worked hard at putting himself in, or near, the scene of the murder. Obviously he was placing his troop of Simms boys there as well, but when it came to anyone who stood high enough to have been able to inflict any of the blows that marked the dead man's body, he had nobody he would give the inspector but himself.

Spotting what seemed to be a loose thread, Inspector Schmidt came at it from that angle.

"You took the kids out by the front room and took them straight home to their mother. Do I have that right?"

Mallard beamed on the inspector.

"You're a good listener," he said. "Good listeners aren't always easy to find."

He was putting on a great act of being blithe and carefree. The act called for lines of just such silly prattle.

"You knew she had left the hospital?"

"I more than half expected she would. You'll never catch Norah staying away from the troops a minute longer than she has to."

"You knew she was home?"

"I took them home because we were hitting toward the time when they get sleepy. Pretty quick after they get sleepy they cork off, and then they have to be carried. I had the baby to carry anyhow and I can manage one more. All of them is too much. The trick is to get them bedded down when they're just ready for it but while they can still make it that far on their own feet. You can understand that, I'm sure."

"I'm a good listener. You said you took them home to their mother, not that you took them home to bed."

"Yes, yes, yes. I see. I see."

The big clown was happy as larks. He had caught on to what was bothering the inspector, and he was being every inch the good guy who liked nothing better than being able to relieve the inspector's mind. With that painstaking precision he had been bringing to all of those narrowly limited memories of his, he lined it out.

At the time he had marched his company of small boys out of Dinah's by way of the front room, he'd had no way of knowing whether he would find their mother at home waiting for them. He had been fully prepared to take the boys home, bathe them, put them into their pajamas, and tuck them in. He gave the inspector a step-by-step rundown on the whole process, even to telling him that *in loco parentis* he would have kissed them good night, but then he

explained that when he got home with the kids, he'd found Norah there waiting for them. They'd split up between them the job of getting the boys tucked in for the night.

"Right out of hospital," he said, "it was better for her not to undertake too much. Also there are limits to even what a competent woman like Norah can do this soon after she's been kicked in the belly. She'll be needing help for a while, at least till her ribs are healed."

We could have gone on that way indefinitely. Mallard showed not the first sign of running out either of words or of his own brand of eager helpfulness. He had, however, no intention of giving the inspector anything, and the chance of trapping him into letting anything slip seemed to me too slim to be worth pursuing. I had for some time been looking for some sign that Inspector Schmidt might be ready to pull out. Such sign might have been about due, but just then we had a diversion.

In any tenement, the walls between flats are thin. It takes no electronic aids to carry sound through them. Privacy is one of the many luxuries unavailable to the poor. Through the wall that separated the Mallard flat from the Simms flat, there came the sound of a baby's crying. It was a lusty wail. Mallard broke off in midsentence. Almost as quickly as the crying had begun, it broke off.

"That's Danny," Mallard said. "She's picked him up."

A stream of small murmurings came through the wall. I can't say I recognized the voice, but I could tell it was neither an infant nor a child. It was an easy guess that it would be Norah Simms and that she was cooing softly, half talking to herself and half making soothing sounds for her baby's comfort.

Mallard headed for the door.

"Since it's Danny," he said, "you can bet he'll need changing. I've got to go do it. You hang on here. I'll be

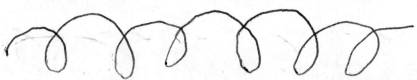

back in a minute. I'm a talented guy, and this is one of my
specialties."

"We know," I said. "We've seen you perform."

"We could go with you," the inspector suggested.

"You haven't been asked," Mallard said. "It's the wrong
time for it. The lady's in no shape for receiving visitors.
Also it's no good barging in there and waking the rest of
the kids. Danny will cork right off again, but I know the
rest of them. They'll be up and roaring, and not tonight.
Tonight she needs her rest."

The inspector took the turndown without a murmur.
Maybe he was conceding the justice of Mallard's objections, or possibly even he was coming to the place where,
like the lady, he might have needed his rest. I was well past
the place where I'd begun needing mine.

The big boy took off. Trotting out, he carefully shut his
door behind him. We could hear him go the few steps down
the hall, and we could hear him open the Simms door. We
heard her protests. She was going to have to manage for
herself. He couldn't come running over every time the kid
cried.

His answer was even more audible than her words had
been.

"Why can't I? I'm as good a man as your Danny is. Any
time he can wet, I can run. You go back to bed and leave
him to me."

And that was all. What followed was silence. A few minutes later, however, another sound came to us. This new
one wasn't from the flat next door. It was from the direction of the hall. It came from just outside Mallard's door.
More precisely it came from the door itself. It was the
grating of a key in the lock. My first thought was it would
be Mallard coming back, even though it was too quick even
for a man of his demonstrated talents.

I should, of course, have remembered that, on going out, Mallard had merely drawn the door shut after him. He hadn't stopped to turn any key in any lock. I should also have observed that the door was not fitted with any sort of snap lock. Since he hadn't locked it and it couldn't have locked itself, the turning of the key could hardly mean that it was now being unlocked.

Need I tell you that Inspector Schmidt did remember and had observed? Even while I was expecting Mallard to come back in, having set a new record for diaper changing, the inspector was jumping for the door. He was, of course, too late. The door had been locked from the outside.

He tried it and promptly came away from it. Either one of us could have put a shoulder to it and crashed it open. Tenement doors are a match to the walls, flimsy. The inspector, however, had other ideas. He tiptoed to the wall and pressed his ear against it, listening for sounds from the Simms flat. I edged up beside him and took up my own listening post.

Nothing was coming through. It was dead silence. The quiet, however, lasted only a short time. It was broken first by small sounds, a cautious bout of door rattling. Then there was a period of muttering. Breaking off after a few moments, it was followed by some discreet tapping on the wall to which we had our ears pressed.

"We're here," the inspector said. "We're listening."

Mallard began talking through the wall. He was keeping his voice down. It came through as little more than a murmur, but it was an audible murmur.

"She's gone back to bed and she needs it," he was saying. "She's asleep already and Danny was asleep before I'd finished changing him. I'm holding it down. I don't want to wake them."

"Someone's playing games," the inspector said.

"I know. Some clown crept up on Norah's door while I was busy with Danny. He's locked it from the outside. I'm locked in here and I will be until I can get Norah's key. Big, big, funny, funny joke. I'm not going to go fumbling around, looking for her key because I'll be a sure shot to wake them all up, and I don't need that. I can sleep over here. I'm all right without a bed. I just stretch out on the floor. I like floors. So I'm sorry. No more tonight. Tomorrow I'll be at your disposal. It can be here or I can come down to your office, though I'll probably have to bring the troops or at least some of them. Norah can't be left to cope with all of them alone, but that's all right. They've already been there without tipping over the scales of justice. So whichever way you want it if you do want it."

"Where do you keep the key to your door?"

"On my key ring. Here in my pocket. Where would I keep it?"

"Some place that could be more convenient right now. Your clown has also locked your door."

"He's no clown of mine," Mallard began. He broke it off as the inspector's meaning percolated through. "You mean you're locked in there just like I'm locked in here?"

"Got it on the first bounce."

Mallard snickered.

"It is funny," he said. "But Chief of Homicide, that's *lèse majesté* or something. How many years in the pokey is it for lèse majesté?"

"Okay. Enough with the wit. How are you going to get us out of here?"

"Easy. As soon as Norah's up, I'll get her key. That turns me loose and first thing, even before breakfast, I'll come over and unlock the door for you."

"Come morning?"

"Come morning unless she gets the good sleep she needs

and isn't up till afternoon. There's only the one bed. Sorry about that, but it's a big bed, easily big enough for two. Ask any of the people who have shared it with me. Help yourself to anything you need. If you get hungry, there's the instant cocoa."

"Not morning," the inspector said. "Now. Right now."

"Oh, come on!" Even filtered through the wall, his murmur dripped disgust. "Impatience gets you nowhere. Try a little resignation."

"Want us to crash out? We can and easy."

"Not with my consent. The landlord won't like it, and you're not sticking me with paying for any repairs. Look, can't you take a joke?"

"What makes you think it's a joke, or is that what you're trying to sell me?"

"What else can it be?"

"We're getting out to check on just that. If it isn't a joke, we're not waiting till morning to find out what it is."

Up to that point Inspector Schmidt had been playing along—holding his voice down, not waking anyone unnecessarily, going along with Dan Mallard on that character's definition of necessity. Now he was making the abrupt switch to what he himself considered to be necessary. Doubling up both fists, he pounded on the wall. Along with his pounding, he shouted. He was making enough noise to rouse up the whole building, but he was yelling for Norah Simms. She had the key that would spring Dan Mallard to come back and let us out.

Whether she woke immediately under the pounding and shouting, or whether her waking was delayed by a moment or two, there was no way of knowing. It was only a moment, after all, that the inspector was alone in his thunderings. Everybody woke and everybody gave voice. From every side there came at us mighty roars of "SHADDAP."

From most directions there came as well an assortment of
epithets and genealogies that quickly went beyond the cus-
tomary allegations about Inspector Schmidt's mother.

The shouted insults, however, were the least of it. The
whole tribe of Simms kids woke and made their own deaf-
ening contributions to the chorus. Obviously their mother
couldn't sleep through all that. She apparently did try or
perhaps she lay doggo in the hope that, if she ignored it, it
might go away. There was also the possibility that she
hadn't been asleep at all but had been taking a hand in the
games playing.

In any case it seemed a long time before we heard her
voice come cutting through the caterwauling beyond that
common wall. That would be it. The inspector had accomplished his objective. The lady was awake. She would let
Mallard out of her place. He would come and let us out of
his. The inspector fell silent and waited.

We could hear through the wall as Dan and Norah went
about the task of silencing her battalion of tots. The process couldn't be called instantaneous. It wasn't even quick.
Voice by voice they shrank the chorus and, with the dimin-
ishing noise level, the neighbors also began dropping away.
We could now hear through the wall what Norah and Dan
were saying one to the other.

She wanted to know what the hell was going on. She also
wanted to know how Mallard happened to be in her place.
Hadn't he gone back to his own flat? She sounded confused
and bewildered. Mallard explained. Some clown had
locked the doors, and the inspector was an inconsiderate
bastard who just for a small inconvenience had roused the
whole neighborhood.

"If he thinks I'm going to let him out, he's crazy. Maybe
I'll go soft in the morning and let him out then, but now

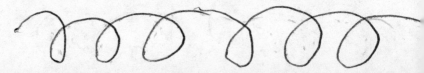

I'm thinking I'll just go off and forget about him. He can stay there and rot."

Norah protested.

"And we get no sleep?"

This exchange was spoken right up against the wall. Obviously it was intended for the inspector's ear. Obviously, however, he could also play at that game. He moved in on the wall.

"Okay, Baggy," he said. "How long do we give him before we crash out of here?

I nuzzled the wall along with him.

"Why give him any time? He's earned the repair bill."

"We can ram his table against the door, and it'll give," the inspector said. "No need for us to beat up on our shoulders."

Mallard said nothing. It was Norah who spoke.

"Hold it," she said. "Dan's crazy, but I'm not." She broke off and we could hear her speak to Mallard. "Give me your key," she said.

"What for?"

"So I can get them out of there, you idiot. So we can have a little peace around here tonight. What else for?"

"That inspector needs a lesson."

"The hell with that. I need sleep."

Mallard grumbled. He agreed to unlock his door. I think he had even come around to welcoming the idea. He now had the opportunity to hurl at the inspector face to face some assiduously elaborated epithets we just might have missed hearing through the wall. He had hardly more than begun on them, however, before Norah Simms came out to the hall to shut him up.

"They heard you the first time, Danny," she said. "You can also do it all over for them in the morning. You won't forget any of it. You may even think up some new words,

but for Christ's sweet sake give it a rest now. I can't take any more tonight, Danny. Let's all simmer down. Please?"

She wasn't exaggerating. If I have ever seen a woman worn to the last frayed thread of endurance, I was seeing one then. The lady looked awful. Her whole body was sagging. It could have been nothing but the white-knuckled grip of her hand on the door to her flat that was keeping her upright. The only color that showed in her face was the dark of the rings under her eyes. They were more than rings. They were on the way to taking over halfway down to her chin.

So Mallard let it go with telling us that he was aching to kick us down the stairs but that for Norah's sake he was controlling himself. He suggested that we get out of there while his control still held. Ignoring his ranting, Inspector Schmidt swept past him. The inspector had something else on his mind, something more important than taking on an exchange of compliments with Mallard the Muscles.

He raced down the stairs. I was at his heels. I expected we'd be going straight on out the front door, but downstairs the inspector headed the other way. At the ground-floor rear the old lady's door now stood ajar. Across the doorstep lay our ancient harridan. It occurred to me then that in the chorus of vituperation I'd not heard her voice. The inspector, of course, had been way ahead of me there.

She again had that wrecked electric iron with her. At first glance I thought that, swinging it at someone, she had, through some peculiar mismanagement, knocked herself out with it. When we came close enough to stand directly over her, however, that possibility eliminated itself.

The old woman was dead. She had been killed with her own weapon. Someone had found a method more effective than her wild swings. The iron itself had been bypassed. Only its cord had been put to lethal use. Whipped around

her throat, it had been jerked tight. The lady had been garrotted.

Inspector Schmidt touched the body. He wasn't feeling for any remaining faint pulse of life. It was too late for that. The electric cord was still tight around her neck, and nothing can bite into a throat that deeply without doing an irreversibly lethal job.

"Still warm," he said.

It seemed to me that it stood to reason. She had been much alive when we'd left her to go upstairs. Despite Dan Mallard's garrulity, we hadn't been up there so long that, even if death had come to her almost immediately after we'd left her, there could have been time enough for the body to have lost the last of its living heat.

"We weren't upstairs as long as it might have seemed," I said.

"And we were locked in only a short time. She hasn't even begun to go cold, and it's only minutes before the first signs of cooling begin to show up."

"So it was after the door was locked on us?"

The inspector nodded.

"This much accomplished in that short time," he said. "No telling what could have been done with the rest of the night if we'd accepted the big clown's hospitality."

"It's mugging technique," I said. "Would you have thought she had anything worth taking?"

"She had her life."

"Of value to her. To anyone else? Why? For what gain?"

"You ask good questions, Baggy."

"Got any good answers?"

"Not yet, but I'm going to have to develop them. It could be we made it easier for her killer by our tangling with her first."

I could have preferred that the inspector not bring that up. It was uncomfortable and an unhappy thought. I was recalling the old woman's second effort. It hadn't been much. For the old it takes time to come back. Her killer would have had it far too easy. He had disposed of an exhausted and enfeebled old woman.

I sighed.

"Tangling with us took too much out of her."

The inspector shrugged.

"That wouldn't have made the difference," he said. "What she had in her before she tangled with us could never have been enough. It's just that after one false alarm —just the two of us instead of the man she'd been expecting —she had just that much edge taken off her alertness when the real thing did turn up a few minutes later."

"She had been expecting someone in particular? Not the way she said? Not muggers in general?"

"Muggers catch their victims out in the hall. They don't break down doors to get at them. She was expecting someone."

"And it wasn't a rapist?"

"What do you think?"

VI.

Her name was Henrietta Blau. She had been the building's oldest tenant. As far as any living memory ran, she had always lived in that ground-floor rear. In the other flats, tenants came and went but Henrietta Blau had been a fixture. She had also been a loner.

In a setup where nobody could expect much in the way of privacy, she had managed always to keep to herself. She had never had anything for her neighbors but contempt, insult, and curses. She had been the house snob, drawing a class distinction between herself and the other tenants and rubbing it in on them at every opportunity. She was upper class. They were scum.

With Dan Mallard she had shared the distinction of not being a welfare client. She had been a garment worker for more than fifty years and had retired on social security and her union pension. It's a strong union and it's been around a long time. Its pensions are good, and it has a great range of benefits for its people.

Like Dan Mallard, therefore, she had lived where she did through choice and not from necessity. She could have afforded better. She had, however, been a miser and a misanthrope. She hadn't had a friend in the house, and her neighbors were of the belief that she had never had a friend anywhere.

It was to have been expected that nobody in the building would know anything. People who live as they do, under an unremitting threat of violence, make it a matter of prin-

ciple to know nothing. In this case of the murder of Henrietta Blau, however, I had the feeling that none of these people who had known her cared much either. A few did summon up a perfunctory sort of regret, but even that sounded forced. Nobody went so far as to say that the house was well rid of the old bag, but no few of them let you sense such a trend in their thinking. Horror of the way she had died and fear of what appeared to be loose along their halls seemed to be the sum of what the neighbors were feeling.

For Captain Wishes Leary's boys, this one did provide some small variation from their weary expectations. They had all had far too much of the job of seeking out witnesses among people who never heard anything and never saw anything. For this once, it was different.

Nobody had seen anything. That part of it ran to pattern, but everybody was ready to give detailed testimony to what he heard. There had been violence. There had been uproar. There had been pounding and shouting. The whole neighborhood had been wakened. It had been enough to waken the dead.

Unfortunately, it was no more than what we already knew. The uproar had been ours, the inspector's and mine. We could hardly set aside the disquieting thought that all the noise we'd been making in the flat above could have been a screen that had covered any sounds of violence the killing of Henrietta Blau might have produced. This time the neighbors were telling the whole truth of what they'd heard. If there had been any significant sounds, we had drowned them out.

The boys, of course, went through the whole house. They found nothing irregular anywhere. All the occupants had been in their respective flats behind their respective locked

doors. You already know about the exceptions. Dan Mallard had been in the Simms flat behind a locked door. Neither he nor Norah Simms could be moved from their story that it had been locked from the outside by some unknown. No other door in the building had been so treated, but then the testimony from all the other flats had it that their doors had been locked to begin with.

Nobody was missing. All residents of the building were in and all insisted that they had been in well before the night's first noisy disturbance. That one, of course, had been the rumpus Henrietta Blau had raised when she heard us outside her door. Apart from the inspector and myself there had been no visitors, and it was the unanimous testimony that there had been none since well before the time we'd arrived to tangle with the old lady.

If all this was negative, examination of the body and the flat seemed to offer little more. There was every indication that the killing had been quick and efficient. However feisty I had found Henrietta Blau, all the evidence said that later, when she had come up against her killer, there had been none of that.

Enraged with me, she'd made every effort to claw. That she hadn't succeeded much was only because I'd had both hands free for preventive action. Beyond curbing her ferocity, I'd had no other project in hand. Her killer obviously had been in quite another position. Putting the electric cord around her neck and jerking it tight would need to have been a two-hands job and no hands left over to fasten on her wrists and keep her claws out of action.

The inspector's men examined her fingernails for any trace of skin or hair or blood. They found some but, even before the lab reports came through considerably later, I knew they were going to be mine. The best guess was that she had been taken by surprise, meeting death at the hands

of someone with whom at that moment at least she had felt safe. This someone had then turned on her with such speed and efficiency that she'd had not even a moment's time for fighting it.

There was nothing to indicate that she had been robbed. Her flat looked just as it had when we'd been in there earlier that night. There was none of the disorder typical of a place that has been ransacked. Her purse lay on the table. It was closed. When the boys checked, they found money in it. It was no great sum—nineteen dollars and some change, but that was enough to rule out robbery. A thief takes valuables where he finds them, but there is no thief who doesn't prefer the simple, riskless negotiability of cash. In a robbery, other items might have been taken as well, but the cash would not have been left untouched. We pulled out and at long last called it a night.

It wasn't until morning that the inspector was ready to talk about this murder that humiliatingly had been done all but under his nose.

"We came close last night," he said. "The old babe could have saved herself. If she had talked to us, that would have been it."

"Would it? Why knock her off to stop her talking when she was just fresh from demonstrating that she wouldn't talk?"

"Her killer was not impressed with the demonstration. He was taking no chances on her. There's also a good possibility that there's more to her killing than the threat of her later deciding to talk to us."

"Like what?"

"Like she might have been more than a potential witness. She may have been a participant."

"That," I said, "is great for explaining why she wouldn't

talk. It also suggests, though, that talking might have done her no good."

"I could have provided her with protection."

With all due respect for Inspector Schmidt, I was less than impressed with the record the police had been setting up in the protection-of-endangered-witnesses department. Despite their best efforts, they had been losing too many. I winced away from the thought. I didn't have to say anything. Inspector Schmidt was reading me.

"This," he said, "is no gang deal. I'm not going up against the big battalions."

"I wish I knew what you are going up against."

"We'll find out. We're on the way."

"On the way to what?"

"On the way to putting this thing into proportion. The way we've been seeing it—and it may be the way we've been maneuvered into seeing it—it's ridiculously out of proportion. We began with a standard, garden-variety, run-of-the-mill Mothers' Day ripoff. That's not a big enough deal to set off this chain reaction of killings."

I was outraged.

"A pregnant young woman was beaten. Her ribs were kicked in. She's miscarried. You call all that a small thing?"

"I call none of it small, Baggy. You know that. Small is what the ripoff artist would call it. He hit her and ran. It happens all the time and all the time that's an end of it. What made this one different? Why should this one be going on and on?"

"Dan Mallard," I said, feeling my way. "At the outset he made threats. If he caught up with the lug who made the hit on Norah, he wasn't going to need the police."

"Talk," the inspector said. "The man's an actor, and actors are big on role-playing. Roles they get to play on the

job are never heroic enough to satisfy them, so they take to improvising scripts for themselves. They give themselves all the big lines."

That much was all right, but when the inspector went on with it, I was sorry I'd brought it up. I had formed a liking for Dan Mallard.

"Of course, this one," the inspector added, "does TV commercials. They use none of him but his muscles and even those only for selling cocoa, beer and crispy crunchies."

"Nothing heroic there," I said.

"Maybe that's all the more reason for him to compensate off the tube."

"I'd guess the big talk would be all the compensation he needs."

"On the other hand, he has the muscles," the inspector said. "Does his need for compensation run to making more use of them?"

"Then why would he come to you?"

"He didn't come to me. He just sounded off to you. You took it from there."

"He's an actor and actors need an audience. He picked me for it."

"A dangerous pick right there at headquarters. He'd have to be a fool."

"Or a guy who likes to live dangerously."

"He strikes me as not being that simple," the inspector said. "He's an actor and he's on all the time. He has the actor's view of life. He sees it across the footlights and from the stage side."

"What the hell does that mean?"

"People like ourselves, if we think about the theater at all, we see it as a reflection of life. Actors see it the other way around. For them, life is a reflection of the theater."

"An interesting point, but where does it go toward interpreting Mallard's behavior?"

"I'm trying to put myself in the place of a man whose total experience of blood may have been red paint or ketchup. Suppose he's playing this like a murder-mystery script. In the solution of a whodunit, where does the guilt finally fall? Never on the most obvious suspect. We have him role-playing. What says this isn't the role he's picked for himself, most obvious suspect? He could be playing it either way, to cover himself or to cover someone he knows is guilty and whom he wants to protect."

That struck me as overelaborate.

"Nonsense," I said. "If you're a playwright, you want to build suspense. Also you have complete control. No facts will turn up other than those you choose to invent, and you invent the ones that suit your purpose. You rig the thing to fix the guilt on the least obvious suspect. You have to do that if you want suspense, but you're Inspector Schmidt. You don't want suspense. You want the facts. There could hardly be a greater difference."

"Exactly," the inspector said. "I'm just wondering whether Mallard can see it our way. It's clear enough from our side of the footlights. How is it looking from his?"

I tried adding it up. In the event that Inspector Schmidt might have had any doubt of the clean-up in Dinah's back room having been an effort toward elimination of incriminating evidence, Mallard had with the greatest readiness assured him that it had been just that. Obviously he could have gone on from there and, by naming names, have furnished the inspector with a list of potential witnesses and possible suspects. He had chosen instead to give the inspector nobody but himself.

The inspector could, of course, read this area of reticence

for a reflection of the man's exalted moral character. Mendacity and evasion he disdained if they were to be exercised in his own interest. Following, as an adult, some code of behavior he had learned as a schoolboy, he wouldn't lie or remain silent if it was for his own advantage, and equally he would consider it dishonorable to tell the truth where the telling would be to some other man's disadvantage. You didn't tell on anyone. You took the law into your own hands instead.

We all went through that stage at one time or another. Remember? You didn't go running to teacher with tales of another kid's malefactions. You kept an honorable silence and ambushed him in the schoolyard instead where you beat up on him.

It seemed silly. It might well be characterized as a matter of arrested development, but so long as there'd been only the one murder, I'd hardly have been disposed to dismiss it as impossible. The second murder, however, the killing of old Henrietta Blau, was something else again. I could see no way of making that one fit into anybody's schoolboy romanticism. Could the childish code of honor ever have been stretched to include the knocking off of old ladies?

If I couldn't make that picture of Mallard and his involvement stand up, I was hardly more ready to accept the line the inspector had suggested. To say Mallard had with great industry been setting himself up as the most obvious suspect, because he was deluded by a theatrical view of reality, might be to focus only on what Mallard had been saying to the neglect of the possible significance of his reticences and his silences.

He hadn't tried to give us the idea that he and the troop of Simms kids had been the only customers in Dinah's back room that night. He had taken no notice. He didn't remember. Could he be so simpleminded that he would

hope Inspector Schmidt might believe either such inattention or such forgetfulness?

It might well be that with his silence he was accusing all the people who had eaten there that night. By his refusal to name anyone, he was suggesting that the people he had seen in the back room had been there not for Dinah's food but for other purposes. Certainly he could have given us a list of obvious innocents, holding back only such names as the inspector might be expected to pick up as suspects. If you will go along on excepting his squad of small boys, however, he had given the inspector nobody.

"We need to know a lot more about Norah Simms," the inspector said, "and so far we know almost nothing about Henrietta Blau."

I picked up on the latter part of that.

"You think the old lady's killing might be an independent thing? Nothing to do with the bum in the alley and nothing to do with the Norah Simms assault and robbery?"

The inspector grinned at me.

"First," he said, "I'll concede that Henrietta was old. She was no kind of a lady."

I grinned back.

"De mortuis . . . "

"De mortuis," the inspector said. "We've got to do some hard thinking. There was too much phony in that show she put on with us."

"In what respect?"

"It was never self-defense. Self-defense would have given her no reason to open her door. Then she went on and on with it. She went on with it long past the point where it would have been obvious to her that we would do her no harm."

"And why?"

The inspector shrugged.

"One of the many things we need to know."

"Any ideas?"

"Ideas? I need more than ideas. All that noise to alert Mallard and give him time to get set for me? To alert Norah? Or was it for someone else and not for them? Was she getting the word to some unknown that we were in the building? Maybe she was giving him time to get himself out of sight before she turned us loose to go upstairs?"

"If she was herself involved and putting on an act, wouldn't she have been putting it on for our benefit? Isn't that enough?"

"For our benefit she didn't have to work at reaching her wider audience. I see it as an act that had to be heard beyond the walls of her ground-floor rear."

"We don't know anything about her normal voice. Maybe she always shouted."

"You can tell when someone's working at it."

"Then you are going to work on the assumption that both killings are sequelae to the Simms ripoff and not just the one in the alley."

"I'm keeping an open mind. We still don't know that even the first killing was related to the ripoff."

"Oh, come on now! Her ID was found under Blue's body."

"Her ID was found under the body, but just her ID. The money, which presumably would have been what he wanted, wasn't on him, even though it was not only the desirable part of the deal but also the unidentifiable part of it. All that was found with him was the useless and incriminating part of the loot, her ID."

"There had been the whole day since morning," I said. "The money could have been spent. It could have been stashed away someplace. He could have had his turn at being robbed. That doesn't mean a thing."

"It doesn't but the ID does. It means that what we're looking at isn't what happened. It's an appearance that someone took pains to establish."

He lined it out for me and I couldn't find the smallest flaw in his argument. Standard operating procedure in any robbery would have the robber at his earliest opportunity ridding himself of any identifiable object. He would do that first. Spending the money or stowing it away in a safe place would come later.

Work it out for yourself. He hit Norah Simms. He hauled the money out of where she had tucked it. When he unrolled the wad of bills, he found the ID card. Doesn't he rid himself of that immediately?

"Do we then," the inspector said, "assume that Blue was a mugger totally ignorant of the simplest practises of his trade? Do we assume that he hung on to the worthless and dangerous ID, hung on to it with such determination that he wasn't to be separated from it even in death?"

"So he was stupid. It's hard to believe anyone could be that stupid, but evidently this man was. The ID was found with his body."

"You say evidently. Why not apparently?"

"The thing was there with him. It didn't seem to be there. You saw it with your own eyes, Schmitty. What could be more obvious?"

"It was there. That's obvious enough. What isn't obvious is how it came to be there."

I had a ready answer. I had precedents and I cited them. The phenomenon of the considerate crook is by no means unknown. The considerate crook snatches money and any other valuables he might expect will be negotiable. If, however, he happens to grab along with the valuables something that is not only worthless to him but dangerously

identifiable, your considerate crook departs from the procedure other crooks would follow. He doesn't leave it at merely ridding himself of the worthless and potentially incriminating surplus. He's particular about the exact place where he will rid himself of the thing. He drops it where it is most likely to be found by his victim or at least by someone who might be expected to return it to his victim. He has stolen what he wanted, but he does his victim the kindness of returning what he doesn't want—in this case the ID card.

"Dinah's alley," I said. "Norah Simms frequented it. Her friends frequented it. Blue had it picked as a good place to drop the card. People who use that alley are people who know Norah Simms. Someone would find it and return it to her."

Even while I was expounding my theory, I was warming to it. Perhaps I was liking my hypothesis so much because I was finding in it an engaging irony. Here was a man who was getting away with the evil he had done. It had been only his good impulse that had done him in.

"He wanted to drop it where one of her friends would find it," I said. "His timing was unfortunate. One of her friends happened along just as Blue was dropping the ID. The friend dropped him."

The inspector shook his head.

"Most unlikely," he said.

"Tell me why."

"He waited too long. He waited past the time that could have been safest for him, and he went to the alley when it was most dangerous. There are other reasons as well, but let's get this one sewed up first. Any normal procedure would have him ridding himself of the ID at the earliest opportunity, not some twelve hours later. The first hour or two after the mugging would have taken him into the alley

before Dinah opened up for the day. She doesn't do breakfasts."

"Opens at noon?" I asked.

"Eleven-thirty. During the morning, nobody goes through the alley except Dinah and the people she has working for her. They come in early to get things going for opening time. Once they are in, they stay in. They're too busy to be going back and forth in the alley or to be hanging around out there. Otherwise there will be nobody but deliverymen."

"They also would come early," I said.

"Yes. All that activity in the alley was over before the check-cashing agency opened its doors. From the time Norah Simms was hit until a little before eleven-thirty, when the earliest of Dinah's back-room customers might have been turning up for lunch, Blue could have gone into the alley and dropped the card with minimum risk. Would Blue let the quiet time go by to hit it in the rush hour?"

"I suppose not," I said, "but only if he knew as much as you do about normal traffic patterns through the alley. What evidence do you have that he did know? I see a contrary indication. If we believe Dinah, Blue was a person who wasn't welcome in her place. So how could he know when would be a good time and when a bad one?"

The inspector was as ready with his answer as I had been with my question.

"You're assuming he knew enough about the restaurant to know there was a back room, to know it was reached through the alley, and to know that Norah Simms and her friends went there. He needed only to go by the place to see what her opening and closing hours are. He mightn't have had all the information he needed for picking the safest time. I find it hard to believe he didn't have the little information he needed for avoiding the most dangerous hour."

"You said there were other reasons, too."

"The body shows unexplained cyanosis."

"Yes. I saw that."

"The body then for some time after death lay somewhere other than the place we found it."

"Does it need to have been another place? Suppose someone merely shifted the body's position, rolled him over where he lay?"

"In the alley?" the inspector said. "Could the body have lain there dead that long? It would mean it was in the alley a long time, long enough in its first position for the blood to have settled and set up the cyanosis. Then after all that time a character comes along and rolls the body over. Why? Can you go for that?"

As always, the inspector was right. I couldn't. Cyanosis is the blue discoloration we had seen on the body before the body had been touched by any one of us. Such discoloration appears in the parts of a dead body where the blood settles after circulation has stopped with the stopping of the heart. Blood doesn't settle up. I was recognizing all that, but I had another idea.

"How would this work out?" I said. "What you're thinking is that Blue wasn't the mugger. So let's say Blue has been killed. We don't know why or by whom. His body is lying in the alley. The mugger who took Norah's ID card along with her money did toss the card away at the earliest opportunity. In the evening, however, he comes on the body in the alley. He's been worried about the Simms mugging. He's not certain that he got away on that as clean as he would have liked. He sees a possibility of improving his position. He'll set up something in the way of a safeguard."

The inspector picked it up.

"He runs back to wherever it was he had dropped it," he said, obviously inspecting the idea even as he was putting it

into words. "It's still there. He snatches it up and he returns to the body where now for the second time he rids himself of the card. To make sure that it will be connected with the body, he rolls the body over on to it. That makes certain that nobody just in passing might kick it away to the end of the alley and obscure the connection he's gone to so much trouble and risk to establish."

"And there's your time element," I said. "While the mugger is off to retrieve the card, the corpse is lying there developing the cyanosis."

I didn't say QED, but I was thinking it.

Inspector Schmidt, however, moved in on my structure to explode it, but not to destroy all of it. He salvaged a large piece out of the debris.

"No, kid," he said. "It won't hold. You're still stuck with the wrong time of day, too much coming and going through the alley during the time the body would have been lying there developing its cyanosis. The mugger sees the body. He hurries off to retrieve the card and bring it to the alley to relose it. He's gone long enough for the cyanosis to develop. How come the body is still there when he comes back, still there and still unreported? Dozens of people would have passed by and seen it."

"He doesn't have to have been gone that long. When the mugger first came on it, the body could already have been there long enough to develop the cyanosis."

"No difference, Baggy. Either way it would have been lying in the alley too long. Too many people would have seen it. In all that time the body would either have been reported or it would have been hauled out of the alley and dropped elsewhere."

I gave up on it.

"All right," I said. "Then what is the picture?"

"Blue's killer wanted the body found and, when found,

he wanted it to be inescapably attached to the ID card," the inspector explained. "He could have picked any spot where sooner or later people would have been passing and he could have dropped the card there and dumped the body on it. The alley down to Dinah's back room would have been perfect for him, deserted in the morning, busy by late morning—perfect."

"We've already been over that. We know he didn't do it that way."

"Yes, and we're left with the question of why he didn't. Why would he keep the card all through the day? Blue was killed considerably later, long enough before we found him to have developed the cyanosis but only that long. Rigor hadn't even begun to set in when we found the body. If he had been dead all day, it would have been there and noticeable. So we have the card kept all day and the body kept a shorter but still considerable time in a place or places where this mugger and killer expected they wouldn't be found and where they were in fact not found. Why would he take the risks involved and the further risks of moving the body into the alley in the evening, the busiest and the most dangerous time for that operation?"

"Stupid," I said. "An irresolute improviser. It won't be the first time you've come up against a killer who's only been lucky. He's not as bright as you are."

The compliment, such as it was, the inspector let pass unacknowledged.

"It could well be," he said, "the first time I've come up against a killer who would do something that stupid without even what might seem to him a compelling cause. We do better if we assume that he did think he had a compelling cause and that he acted on it. That way we have something to work with."

"As what?"

"He wanted the body found. He wanted it found with the ID card found with it. He wanted more than that. He wanted it found at a time and place where there would be no possibility that Norah Simms wouldn't know about it. That's one approach for us. If we can learn why anyone would want all that, it could lead us to who would want it. The other approach must be through figuring out how it could have been done. Dragging a body through busy streets to deposit it in the alley? We've been thinking of traffic in the alley. We mustn't forget the problem of traffic in the streets. Between the Simms mugging and the time we came on the body, there was no quiet time in the streets."

That latter question he was raising was a tough one. I had no quick thought on that. I left it for thinking about later.

"Mallard," I said. "Mallard knew he would be taking her kids there for their supper. That would mean he would be in a position to tell her about it himself if nobody else did. He could tell her about it with nobody raising a question of how he knew."

"There's a question I have about Mallard," the inspector said. "When we were locked up in his place last night, he suggested no alternative to our staying there all night. He never brought up the possibility of leaving quietly by the window and the fire escape."

I couldn't go for that.

"In all fairness, we can't assume he thought of it. We didn't."

"You didn't. That's because you've never lived in a tenement. You're not that much used to fire escapes. Mallard lives there."

"Did you think of it?"

"I did. I didn't bring it up because I was testing Mallard."

"So you're thinking Mallard?" I asked.

Despite this fire-escape item, on what he then had the inspector wasn't ready to take it that far.

"Who," he said, "we'd best leave open for the present. We haven't explored the family-affair aspect of the two killings."

"What family affair?"

"Only a hunch, but too good to pass up. A corpse named Blue and a corpse named Blau. Do we call it coincidence and wait for the murder of someone named Azurra?"

"A lug born with a German name and he Anglicized it," I said. "That would be something to go on."

"We are going on it," the inspector said.

VII.

The Blue-Blau angle the inspector left for his Homicide detectives to check out. If there was a relationship and none of Henrietta Blau's neighbors had ever had even the first suspicion of it, then it would need to have been something she and Blue had been keeping well covered up. Uncovering could take a considerable amount of digging but, formidable or not, it would still never be more than a job of routine research.

Meanwhile Chief of Homicide Schmidt was walking around with a headful of questions. He led the way to where he hoped he might find some answers. We returned to the tenement to talk to Norah Simms. I can't say she looked like a new woman. The marks of pain and exhaustion—virtually all one could see of her the night before—hadn't left her. It was obvious that she had slept neither much nor well, but, nonetheless, pain and exhaustion no longer made up the whole of her. Her strength had begun to show and her stamina. She had touched bottom and now she was bouncing back.

She was surrounded by her brood, all the kids except the baby. I don't know about the inspector, but for me at least the manner of her greeting couldn't have been more unexpected. I had hardly hoped for a welcome. We found what seemed to be an eager welcome. She had been hoping we'd be around that morning. She was avid for a talk with us.

"I wanted to say what I had to say when we could be alone," she began. Then, recognizing that "alone" was hardly the word for the small-boy mob scene she had swirling around her, she amended it. "I mean," she said, "before big Dan gets back with Danny. They may be gone all day, but more likely it'll just be the morning. Rather than take the chance, I was going to give you another hour before I gave up on you and talked to the cop you've got downstairs in old Henrietta's place. I'd have to hope he wouldn't be too dumb to get it straight."

I tried to sort that out. There was nothing I could do with it that didn't make the woman sound insane. She wanted to talk to the inspector without Dan Mallard knowing. I read that to mean she didn't trust Mallard. So how to explain her letting this guy she didn't trust go off somewhere with her baby?

"Where does Mallard take the kid?" the inspector asked.

"It's not all the time," she said. "It's just today. This is the first time. Dan's working today. He had the call and I knew about it. That's why I couldn't stay on in the hospital. I knew he had to go uptown this morning, and I know Dan. If I didn't get home and take the boys off his hands, he'd cancel out on the job. I couldn't let him do that."

"That's what you thought. It wasn't what he was going to do?"

"You have to know Dan. He's crazy and he's sweet. That's really what I have to tell you."

"And it's important for me to know that Dan Mallard is crazy and also sweet?"

"I don't want you thinking he could do anything bad."

Evidently it was important to her.

"Even if he is?"

"Because he isn't," she said. "Because he never has and he never will. He couldn't if he tried. He's not like that at all. He's good. He's the best person I've ever known. It's hard to believe anybody could be that good."

Mallard had scolded her for leaving the hospital. He'd insisted that looking after her boys when he went uptown to flex the muscles for the cameras would have been no problem. He'd explained that doing TV was 99 per cent waiting around and 1 per cent working time. It would have been only during that working 1 per cent that he would have needed to enlist someone else for looking after them. He had assured her that there would always be a host of available people, actors sweating out their waits, secretaries, page boys.

"Even with me here," she said, "he insisted on taking Danny with him. He said he wants the producers to see the child. They have a talcum-powder account coming up. He says he wants to sell them on using him diapering Danny. It would be money for him and money for me, but I doubt it. He just dreamed that up to get me to let him take Danny off my hands to give me an easy day. He knows how to get his way with me. He tells me I'm doing *him* the favor, helping him land a job he wants."

The inspector chuckled.

"I wouldn't be too sure," he said. "We've seen him with the safety pins. It's a great act. I've never caught anything that good on TV."

"Yes," she said. "Dan's the greatest."

"Is that all you wanted me to know? Why you were in a hurry to leave the hospital?"

"Where I went when I left the hospital," she said.

"I'm listening."

"I came here."

"What Mallard said you did."

"But he didn't say he wasn't here and the kids weren't here and I knew where they would be."

"And you went there?"

"I went there."

"Before Blue's body was found or after?"

"Before. I was the one who found it."

"Touch it?"

"Me? I had no rubber gloves with me."

"That means you didn't?"

"That's what it means."

"You recognized him?"

"If you're asking did I see it was Blue's body and I didn't touch it because I have some special reason for not messing around with any body of his, then the answer is no—more or less no."

The inspector grinned at her.

"It wasn't what I was asking," he said. "I was asking only a piece of it. Of course, I was going to follow it by asking all the other pieces, piece by piece. You see, that way I could have simple questions and simple, yes-or-no answers. More or less no isn't much good to me."

She explained her "more or less."

"To you," she said, "to Leary, to all the law from top to bottom I'm an unmarried mother who never was married and who never let it stop her from having kids. If I was rich —not just rich enough to be off welfare but rich enough to have the right to be anything I wanted to be—if I was that rich, I could go around doing things without ever having to ask myself what the police will think. The way I am, I don't have to ask myself either. I know what the law will think. It will think the worst. So, if I stumble over any dead bodies, I walk around them, and that's the way it was with the body in Dinah's alley last night. I didn't recognize him. Later when they told me who it was, I had to figure that if I'd stopped to look closer, I might have recognized him. He is somebody I'd been seeing around, but that's all. . . . "

The inspector moved in to wrap it up.

"Then your 'more or less no' means you didn't touch the

body, but you avoided it not because you recognized it for Eddie Blue's body or even for the body of the man who mugged you. You didn't touch it on general principles. You just don't mess around with corpses."

"Something like that," she said. "I didn't recognize him. I wouldn't have touched him if I had recognized him. Somebody I liked, somebody I cared about, maybe I wouldn't stop to think about how the law would look at what I was doing. I'd check him for a heartbeat, check for breathing, try to help even when it was too late."

"But since it was Blue who got no more than was coming to him, you didn't care?"

"We've all got it coming to us. Every last one of us is going to die sometime," she said. "But sometime. Nobody's got it coming to him that he should be hurried into it before his time."

It might have been that she was lecturing the inspector, but it sounded more like a meticulous wariness. The words in her mouth were going to be her own. Nobody was going to be putting anything there.

"There are people I care about," she said, "and there are people who don't matter to me one way or the other. There are also people I don't like. Seeing him dead, I had nothing special against him. He was just somebody who didn't matter much to me one way or the other. I didn't recognize him, but it wouldn't have made any difference if I had. He would still have been somebody who didn't matter much to me one way or the other."

"Even if he was the man who made the hit on you yesterday morning?"

"I didn't know that until later, not till the cops told me they found my ID with the body."

"They say you didn't want to believe it."

The inspector was so beautifully casual about the way he

slipped it in that I knew at once it was the question he had
been holding in readiness all along, too important a question to be asked any other way. It had to come as it did—
by-the-way, suggested only by her mention of the ID card.

It couldn't make even the faintest show of carrying any
weight, certainly nothing like the weight I could sense the
inspector was attaching to it. I was aware of all this, of
course, only because I know the man so well and I've had
so long an experience of the way he works. I couldn't imagine that she could be seeing past his surface manner. Even
now I don't know that she did. It could have been just a
further refusal of words anyone might put into her mouth.

"I had trouble believing it. That's not the same thing."

"You had trouble believing it," the inspector said,
adopting her choice of words and acting as though he considered her way of putting it synonymous with his own.
"Why? What made it so hard to believe?"

"Dope," she said. "They doped me up in the hospital. I
wasn't more than half myself when I split out of there. I
had trouble believing what the cops were telling me because my head wasn't hitting on all six cylinders. Even at
my best I don't have one of your super-eight-cylinder
heads. Last night I was only just barely chugging along."

"Today you're doing all right?"

"Today my head's my own again."

"But still not up to understanding why you had trouble
believing the police had your ID card?"

"I was sure it was in my drawer. I couldn't believe it
would be in two places at once."

"You'd been out to cash your check. Wouldn't you have
needed it for that?"

"No," she said. "They know me. I don't have to show
anything. If I did, the card wouldn't be any good. It doesn't

prove anything. It's just a card I wrote my name and address on."

"Right. So the main idea of having an ID card is to keep the thing on you all the time. In case of accident or sudden illness it helps for informing your next of kin."

She chuckled.

"They're my next of kin," she said, indicating her clutch of little boys. "If they were informed, do you think they'd understand?"

I'd been wondering where the inspector thought he could be heading with that kind of question. It wasn't as though we hadn't seen the ID card. The "who should be informed in case of accident" section was blank. She had never filled in that part of it. I had noticed that much, and I had a clear memory of having noticed it. I couldn't believe that the inspector had been less observant or more forgetful.

"Their father," he said. "He'd be old enough to understand."

Whatever amusement her chuckle might have reflected was knocked off by that comment. Her response was grim, even bitter.

"He," she said, "would be hard to find."

"Dan Mallard?"

"Dan isn't their father."

"I know. He's their baby-sitter, your mother's helper."

"A friend and a neighbor, the best friend anyone could ever have and the best neighbor."

"And when something does happen to you, as for instance yesterday, it's Mallard who takes the boys on. Wouldn't you want him informed so he'd know they need him?"

She gave that careful thought before she ventured an answer.

"It would be nice," she said. "The way it was yesterday

didn't matter. The kids were already with him. It would be for times maybe when I had them out with me. If anything happened to me then and it wasn't here in the neighborhood where people know us, it would be for then."

"But you never thought of it?"

"I did think of it. . . . "

She was letting it trail off unfinished. The inspector wasn't ready to let it stand at that.

"And?"

She took a little time to study the inspector. It was evident that she was trying to decide whether or not she wanted to say anymore. After a couple of moments she had decided.

"What the hell!" she said. "Who am I kidding? I'm a welfare mother. I get mother-of-dependent-children benefits. That means I've got the kids to support. I can't go out and work because there's nobody to take care of them, and I don't have a man who can be held responsible for their support or for mine. Give the welfare people even the faintest smell of a man they could try to call responsible and I'm in trouble and he's in trouble and the kids would be going hungry. I have nobody. I'd have to be a fool to go carrying around a card that might give someone the idea that I do have somebody."

"If that goes for Dan Mallard, it would go at least double for their father."

"Except that he's hard to find and Dan isn't."

"Let's get back to your ID card. Without the who-to-inform part, it's useless. You'd be just as well off without it. There's no point in carrying it around on you. It's just as well left in a drawer or even put out with the trash."

She shook her head.

"The day can come when I will need it," she said. "Things can always change."

"But so far they haven't?"

"So far they haven't."

"Then you weren't confused last night when you thought you had it here in the drawer where you always keep it."

"I could have sworn it was there, but of course I was confused because we all know it wasn't there. Blue had it or by that time you people had it because you found it on Blue's body."

"Not on," the inspector said. "Under."

"No difference. He had it anyway, and that has to mean I did have it on me when I was mugged. It can't mean anything else. He got it when he mugged me."

"Even though you never carried it around with you? Even though you always left it in the drawer?"

"I was so confused that I forgot that this time I didn't leave it. I forgot that I'd started carrying it just in case."

"And now you remember?"

"They had me all doped up. Last night I couldn't think."

"It seems a strange coincidence that just this once you should have had the card on you and never otherwise," the inspector said. "We always have to take a good, hard look at strange coincidences. It's always possible that they aren't what they seem to be."

"Okay," she said. "Take your look. You'll see how I cooked up the whole thing. I went out yesterday knowing I was going to get ripped off. I set it up to get myself kicked in the belly. It's a real cheap abortion, isn't it? And I get double benefits this time except for the split I have to make with the guy I hired to rip me off. But I'm doing better than that. I mash his head in and I keep the money all for myself. I think of everything. I take the ID with me and I roll the money around it so when he grabs the money, he'll grab the ID along with it. That way, if when I'm killing him, I run out of luck and I get caught, there'll be proof

that he was the one who ripped me off and I was only trying to get back what he stole from me. Then where do you
go to find a jury that'll convict me?"

The inspector laughed.

"Beautiful," he said. "You should be in my business.
You have a talent for it. So now that you've taken my
good, hard look for me, suppose you take one for yourself
and tell me what you come up with."

"I talk too much, but I began it, so maybe I'd better
finish it. I always kept the card in the drawer. I never bothered to carry it around with me. I thought I didn't need it.
Then these last months—I was pregnant and I thought
maybe I'd be out with the kids and all of a sudden go into
labor. If I had the card on me, people would find it and
know to take the kids to Dan."

"You don't have him on the card."

"I have my name and address on it. They bring the kids
here and Dan's here—or if he isn't, one or another of the
neighbors will look after them till Dan comes in."

"And you just forgot that in this pregnancy you'd made
that change in your habits?"

"That's right. Maybe it's not the way anyone else's mind
works, but mine works that way. I'll put something away
and forget where I put it. I always have to put things back
exactly where I've always kept them. Last night I just forgot that I wasn't leaving it home anymore."

"That was for when you were out with the kids, but yesterday you'd left them with Mallard."

"Who said I didn't have the card with me anyway?"

"Nobody, but even with your new way of doing things,
yesterday wasn't one of the times you'd have been carrying
the card on you."

That she just laughed off.

"With my lousy memory?" she said. "If every last time I

went out I made a decision about whether I'd take it with me or not, I'd be forgetting it most of the time. I just started carrying it on me all the time. That way I couldn't forget."

There it was, and it had all the earmarks of a story she had developed as she went along. Each time she'd tried to stretch it as far as it had to go, it had developed thin spots. Each of those she had then covered quickly with an improvised bit of patchwork.

I expected that the inspector would be right in there to break her down, but that was the moment when we had a diversion. Since it was a diversion that opened up interesting possibilities, it drove straight out of my head any concern with this story Norah Simms had been trying to sell.

You might think that the inspector was similarly turned away from the line of inquiry he had been pursuing, but that would be to underestimate Inspector Schmidt. He did let it drop, but only for the best reasons. He had the answers he had been after.

The diversion was provided by Dan Mallard. It was at that moment he arrived on the scene, bringing the baby home to his mother.

He knocked at the door, but his knock had come while Norah had still been speaking. She delayed going to the door long enough to get the rest of her words in. She was not letting herself be interrupted by anything before she had finished pinning down the last of what she had been trying to feed the inspector.

She might have done better if she had left her thought incompletely spoken and had gone to the door in immediate response to the knock. As it was, she didn't have to open the door to Mallard. Even as she was turning away from us, big Dan unlocked the door and opened it for himself.

We watched him as he came in. We watched him as he turned to take his key out of the lock. It was on his key ring. He saw us and he stopped short. His hand with the keys in it was on its way to his pocket. On his first impulse he stepped up the speed of that hand's movement. He was going to hurry the ring of keys out of sight in the hope that the inspector hadn't noticed. Quickly, however, he was having second thoughts. He brought his hand back up to dangle the keys in front of us. For emphasis he shook the key ring, jingling the keys.

"Truth and consequences," he said. "Twenty questions. Third degree and whatnot. Choose your game, gentlemen, and we'll play it. I do promise I'll play, but business before fun and games. I'm bursting with news and it will take me only a minute to unload it." He turned to Norah. "Baby," he said, "did we ever put it over, Danny and me? All kinds of new vistas opening up and all with Danny. I'm nowhere without him. Disposable-diaper drumbeatings. Talcum-powder pitches. Baby-food buildups. They're setting up a pilot and we're a cinch for a flock of lovely, fat contracts; but, even without looking ahead, we get paid for doing the pilot. And it's only the beginning. Like in the old song they keep asking—'Are there any more at home like him?' It can be there'll be work for all seven of us kids."

She couldn't believe it. He had to convince her. They were much longer kicking it around than his promised minute, but the inspector lay back and let them enjoy it. It took time because Norah Simms was slow about coming around to belief. It was obvious that she had to come to it by pushing past too many other things she had on her mind, worrying things and frightening things.

Her worries, moreover, had to be only part of it. Even if this news had come to her in the best of times, she would in all likelihood have been slow to believe. She had all that it

might ever have taken to cope with adversity. Misfortune was her milieu. It was what she knew. She had the experience and the skills for living with it. In her world there had been no such thing as good fortune. She was going to have to learn how to live with that.

Eventually, however, they put it away and they came back to the inspector. It was Norah who initiated the move.

"Great," she said, "but with you and me tucked away in the lockup, will they use Danny all on his own?"

"Lockup?" Big Dan's happy grin was pushing his beard and mustaches out to new extremes of flamboyance. "We can explain everything."

"Start with the key," the inspector said.

"The key. My key to Norah's door. Her key on my key ring. The key I didn't have last night to let myself out of here so I could get to my door and turn you loose. Is that what you wanted explained?"

"We'll listen to your story."

Mallard sighed.

"Oh, ye of little faith! That's what they are, Norah. They're men of little faith."

"You were about to explain," the inspector said.

"Easy. Once bitten, twice shy. Or maybe it's the other way around. I was shy the key last night, so here I'm bitten by it today. That's the worst of the old saws. They look as though they would be applicable, but they never quite fit."

"Like all people who talk too much," the inspector said, "you say too little. Are you telling me that you were shy the key last night?"

"I should think that would have been obvious."

"Caught without the key last night, you learned that you could need it. So this morning you got yourself a key in case something like that should happen again."

"Bingo! The man wins the genuine fourteen-carat-gold thumbscrews."

"And you'll tell me where I'll find the locksmith who made you the key. Since it was only this morning, he won't have forgotten."

"No locksmith," Mallard said. "No new key made. Norah had an extra and she gave it to me. Since it was only this morning, she won't have forgotten."

Norah wasn't waiting to be asked. She shook her head at him.

"Dan," she said. "It's no good. It's silly. Everybody knows you've always had one of my keys. They have only to ask around. The neighbors'll tell them." She turned to the inspector. "The big idiot," she said, "was putting on an act last night. He was trying to protect me."

Mallard's big grin faded. He set to work on another but he didn't get it made. Although he did manage to sustain his light and bantering tone, his face had gone sober.

"Norah is out and it gets to be time for the kids to go to bed. I let them cork off in my place. Then Norah comes home and that means picking them up and carrying them back here. One or another of them is going to wake up and he wakes the rest. Much better for me to bring them over here and get them properly tucked up for the night. Then there's other times. I've got Danny and I run out of diapers. With Danny that's easy to do. I have to be able to get in here for fresh supplies."

"But last night when it was important to move and to move fast, you couldn't use the key and push this explanation at me then?"

"Mind if I take that on piece by piece?"

"If you've got anything to give me that's more than just talk."

"Important to move and move fast," Mallard said, repeating the inspector's words after him. "Let's start with that. I had no way of knowing it was important to move at all, much less move fast. ESP I haven't got. The old bag downstairs was never one of my favorite people, but then I don't like killers either. I walk around up to the navel in prejudices like that. I had no possible way of knowing anything was going on. How would I know it was important to move?"

It had never occurred to him, he insisted, that the game with the locks could have had any sinister purpose. A couple of possibilities had occurred to him. It might have been a simple practical joke. It might also have been someone trying to do him a favor.

"What kind of a favor?" the inspector asked. "Relief from my questioning? Giving you time to work on your story, improve it, put a high polish on it?"

"It could have been that," Mallard said, "even though I didn't need it; or it could have been somebody thinking that locked up in here with Norah all night, I might get her to say yes where she's always been saying no. That would be someone who doesn't understand Norah, but there was you and it's true of you, too. You don't understand Norah. If you knew I had the key, you were going to think it was entree to more than Norah's flat. You were going to think it was entree to Norah's bed."

"So what? It would be none of my business. You told me that much way back when we first met."

"My opinion," Mallard said. "There's no way I can enforce it. What's to stop you making it your business? What's to stop the welfare people from giving her a hard time about this Mallard lug and why isn't he supporting her."

Norah backed him up.

"It's crazy," she said. "We know it's crazy and maybe you know it's crazy, but that's what life is like this side of the tracks."

"Either side of the tracks," the inspector said, "it can be a good idea to put a limit on the number of keys you spread around. Our friend, Dan, has a key and for the best reasons. Who else?"

"Nobody else. I don't spread them around."

She said it flatly, with no show of indignation. She was on public assistance. She was used to such questions. She was long past insult.

"You had your key in here with you last night. Mallard had his on his key ring and the key ring was in here with him. He had it in his pocket. So who was out in the hall to lock your door from the outside?"

"I don't know," she said, "and don't you think I like it. We were talking about it this morning. I thought I ought to have the lock changed, but Dan says that's no good. It's too easy to get keys to these cheap locks."

"What she needs," Mallard said, "is a good lock, not this crap the landlord provides. I've known all along the locks were no good, but it didn't seem to matter because the doors aren't any good either. A baby with a butter knife could break in here or over at my place. But if it's going to be something crazy like last night, a good lock might help. I wanted to have one put on for her, but here we are again— the facts of life this side of the tracks. Her welfare bitch will come visiting and right off where did she get the lock and who paid for it and what else is he paying for?"

"What about keys to your place?" the inspector asked.

Mallard shrugged.

"Who knows?" he said. "Who did I give one to? Nobody. Who has one? I don't know. Anybody. Just on what happened last night, it'll be the same guy as has a key to

Norah's lock. He got that without her giving it to him or knowing he had it. He has a key to my place without my giving it to him or knowing he had it. Maybe he also has a key to the old babe's place downstairs without her ever giving it to him or knowing he had it. Maybe he has keys by the bushel basket or maybe he travels light—just one master key. If you find out, I wish you'd tell us."

VIII.

Wishes Leary had his detective squad working with the inspector's men. They were handling a variety of angles. Interrogation of the other tenants in the building was one of their tasks. I had half expected that the inspector wouldn't be content with leaving it in their hands. I'd been anticipating endless sessions of repetitive frustration. To my astonishment and my pleasure, however, he declared himself to have had all he wanted of that by the time we'd pulled away from Norah Simms and Dan Mallard.

"We worked on too many of them last night," he said. "It gets boring listening to lies and it's even more boring when it's predictable lies. Anyhow we've something more important to do."

That, of course, was the nub of it. We had something more important to do. Boredom would never turn Inspector Schmidt away from a line of questioning he could think might hold even the smallest promise.

"We've got to hand it to the lady, though," I said. "When Mallard started lying to you, she chopped him down quick enough."

"Devotion to the truth? Noble abhorrence of mendacity? Maybe, but don't count on it. All I can hand her is that she's bright enough to sidestep the feeble lie. If you've got one that's going to be blown wide open under the first hard look, you get rid of it quick before it tarnishes the credibility of the lies you can make stand up."

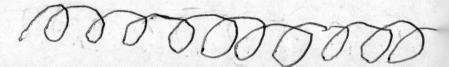

What he was saying was true enough, but I was still left with some admiration for the lady.

"She didn't pretend to nobility," I said. "She couldn't have been more open about it. She just told him to come off it because it wasn't good enough."

"Maybe she was taking no chances on Mallard misunderstanding. She didn't want him to read the signals for anything like they weren't going to lie to me anymore. She maybe had to make it clear to him that they were not giving up on any lies they could keep afloat."

And all along there was something more important that we had to do. Inspector Schmidt had taken off from the tenement at his most purposeful pace. He obviously had a precise idea of where we were going and he was heading for it by the shortest route. It was always possible, of course, that knowing the neighborhood as I didn't, he might come up with a target I couldn't even imagine.

I suppose I wanted to think that, since the only target areas I knew in the neighborhood were, other than the tenement we'd just left, the precinct station house, the hospital, and Dinah's restaurant. If it was to be one of those, on the direction he was taking it had to be Dinah's, and I could think of nothing he might do over there beyond confronting her with the admissions we'd had from Norah Simms and Dan Mallard. I couldn't see where that would get him anywhere. I was foreseeing another exercise in futility.

"Dinah?" I asked. "Do you think you can break her down?"

The inspector laughed.

"I wouldn't even try," he said. "So Mallard was there and the kids were there and Norah came looking for them and on her way in she found the body. We can't expect Dinah to add anything to that. She was busy cooking and how can we say she wasn't?"

"So what's the next move?"

"The alley. We haven't had a look at the alley by daylight."

"You had good lights in there last night. I'd say you saw all there was to see."

"I think I saw everything I looked at. There are things I didn't look at."

He looked, and I looked with him. All that met my eye was verification for the argument the inspector had thrown at me. We were looking the alley over at just that time of day when he had argued it would have been the safest time for depositing Eddie Blue's remains on Dinah's kitchen doorstep.

It was late morning. We had the alley completely to ourselves. Dinah and her help had come through there hours before and had ever since been fully occupied inside with preparations for the business that would flood in on her when she would open her doors to the lunchtime crowd. Her suppliers had all made their deliveries hours before. This was the alley's quiet time, the lull before the day's business began.

"Okay," I said. "It's just as you predicted it would be, but that still doesn't say you could count on it. At any moment someone could be rushing through here. Dinah sends one of her people out to grab up some last-minute item that had been forgotten."

"Unlikely," the inspector said. His mind was on something else but he was disposing of the thought anyhow. "Dinah," he said, "is not a forgetful type. I can't think of anyone less likely to have that kind of an emergency, but anyhow I didn't claim that this could be an absolutely safe

time. There are no absolutely safe times and there are no absolutely safe places. There's always the unforeseeable wanderer who can blunder in and mess things up. This would merely be the safest time of day for dropping the body here. The time when it was dropped was the most dangerous one. That needs explaining. Otherwise I'd be settling for the theory that I'm up against a killer who all at the same time is the world's dumbest and the world's luckiest."

"Luck runs out."

"I wait for that and it can be I'll be waiting till he gets smart. There's an explanation, and it has to be here."

Since he was standing with his back to the wall against which the body had been lying when we came on it, all of his interest appeared to be focused on the opposite wall of the alley. I couldn't imagine a more ordinary wall. There weren't even any graffiti to give it interest.

It was the side wall of a tenement—simple brick punctuated at regular intervals by windows. For each of the five stories there were three windows, one near the head of the alley, one down near its dead end, and the third one—the middle one—just about opposite where we were standing. Fire escapes ran down the face of the wall, serving the windows near the head of the alley and the ones down near its dead end. The middle windows were without fire escapes.

Of course, there was an explanation and it was most obviously there. The big question was the danger of transporting the body through the busy streets that led to the alley. During the summer, slum dwellers live in their streets. Day or night there is no time when those streets will be empty of people. So there it was.

What had seemed inexplicable about the hour chosen for depositing it in the alley had now become ridiculously simple. For what had evidently been done, one time of the day

had been as safe as any other. Nobody had carried a body anywhere. Behind one of the windows in the line directly confronting us lay the place where Eddie Blue had been killed.

Since all that had been needed for putting the body where it was to be found was that it be picked up and tossed out of the window into the alley, all it had taken was watching at the window for a moment of lull in the alley traffic and in that moment heaving it out. I did have the thought that, pleasant as it might be to have this segment of the inexplicable neatly explained, I could see no way in which it brought the inspector nearer to the answer to the one question that mattered, the question of who. I put the thought from my mind.

"Somewhere in there," I said, "back of one of those windows. . . ."

"Window on the lowest floor."

Inspector Schmidt made it specific.

"Sure?"

"The ID card was thrown out into the alley and the body was tossed out to land on it. To aim it from an upper window and land on target would take too much doing."

"It would take expertise," I said, "and who gets to do enough defenestrations to develop expertise?"

"Pretty unlikely."

"And?" I said.

The inspector's tone told me there would be more.

"And," he said, "the condition of the body. Dropped just a few feet and already limp in death, it would show no marks of the fall. Coming down from any of the upper windows, it would have mashed some in landing. There are no accidental marks on the body. All the damage it shows came from aimed blows."

"Right," I said. "So now it's to find out who lives there."

"I should be that lucky. The guy has got to be brighter than that. It's not going to be who lives, it'll be who lived. I'll take bets on it."

"Disposed of the body last night and promptly skipped." I spoke the thought I'd been trying to suppress.

"Skipped only far enough," the inspector said, "to be on hand to lock us up in Mallard's flat during the second killing—old Henrietta's murder."

"And now he could be anywhere."

"All along he could have been anywhere. He's too smart to have done a killing in his own place. This guy pays house calls. He goes out and kills his victims where they live. Five gets you ten it was Blue who lived here."

I had some doubts.

"You'd think someone would have told us last night. If he was her next-door neighbor, Dinah could hardly have not known that his body was as much under his window as on her doorstep. It could have been the easy way to get over the point she was working so hard at putting across. The crime wasn't committed at her place. It was across the alley."

"That," the inspector said, "wasn't the point she was trying to make. She wanted to convince us that nobody who was in her back room could have been Blue's killer. Also telling us anything at all isn't Dinah's technique. It's Mallard's. By telling us something, he hopes to establish an appearance of openness and honesty. This appearance is supposed to fool us into thinking there's no more he could tell."

"And Dinah?"

"Hers is a different method. She tells us nothing because she takes no chances on the possibility that she might inadvertently hand me a clue. If you say nothing at all, you run no risk of saying the wrong thing."

"Identifying him as the no-good who lived across the alley? What could that open up?"

"Questions. Questions about an undesirable neighbor. Maybe Dinah tangled with him at one time or another. Maybe they had a running feud going. When you have somebody covering up, it's all too easy to make the mistake of assuming that anything that's being covered up is something you need to know. It can always be something totally irrelevant and still something that your witness would rather not have known."

It was an obvious error and I had been falling into it. The inspector wasn't going to say as much. He never does. It's not his way and anyhow he doesn't have to. I get the message.

"We go in and look around," I said.

"I go in," the inspector said. "Just in case I should surprise someone in there, this could be his escape hatch. Once I'm in, I'll come to the window and let you know."

It seemed like good thinking. I stayed where I was, keeping my gaze glued to the strategic window. The inspector trotted off up the alley and out to the street.

As soon as he was gone, I began the thinking that had me standing watch outside that window. It still seemed like good thinking but only as far as it went. So long as we had kept it in terms of the window from which the body had been tossed, the obvious conclusion held up. This would necessarily have been the only possible window. Not only was it in the right position for where we had come on the body, but, more than that, it was the window from which a body could have been tossed quickly and easily. Both of the other lines of windows were obstructed by fire escapes.

The body would first have had to be pushed out to the fire escape. Then it would have been necessary to climb out there with it to heave it up over the rail. Obviously, given a

choice of windows, the easiest window would have been used.

I was beginning to feel, however, that all these assumptions were valid only for pitching the body out of the window. For a man who would be making his escape, the assumptions just might not hold up. Climbing over the window ledge and making the relatively short drop to the alley would be a little quicker than scampering down a fire-escape ladder, but the ladder would be by far the safer. Dropping that way to a paved surface, a man doesn't even have to make a very bad landing to twist an ankle. Then, through having to limp the rest of the way he might have to go, he'd lose far more time than he could have gained by making the drop.

I had no way of guessing what the internal space divisions might have been in that particular tenement. It could have been a place where the flats ran the full depth of the building. In that case, anyone the inspector might surprise in there would have access to any one of the three windows. There was, on the other hand, the other possible pattern, the arrangement we had seen in the building where Norah Simms and Dan Mallard lived. There might be two separate flats behind those windows, a front and a rear.

In that event, of course, there was no knowing to which of the two windows the fire escape would belong. I could be certain of only one thing: that window couldn't give on a third unit. Any such arrangement would be a gross violation of the fire laws.

I decided against trying to guess what I couldn't know. The way I would be best advised to play it seemed obvious. If the inspector surprised somebody inside and that somebody attempted a getaway through the alley, there would be only the two ways he could go: across the alley into Dinah's back room or up the alley to try to lose himself in the

busy street traffic. I could see only one possibility of his getting away from me.

Remaining where I was, with the whole of my attention fixed on the central window, I would be in good position for anyone who dropped from that window. For anyone who came down the fire escape at the blind end of the alley, I would also be well placed, the cork in his bottle. Either for making it into Dinah's place or for running the length of the alley to its street end, he would have to get past me.

What I was leaving uncovered was the third possibility. If he came down the fire escape at the street end of the alley, he could be off and lost in the street crowds before I could come anywhere near him. It seemed obvious, therefore, that I would be most effective if I abandoned that central window and positioned myself instead at the street end of the alley.

Then I could have him, whichever way he came. He couldn't make it to the street without getting past me and, although he could dart across the alley and into Dinah's before I could move back in there to nab him, that would be no help to him. At the street end of the alley I would have command of both his ways out—straight down the alley to the street or through the restaurant to hit the street by way of its front entrance.

It takes longer to explain this than it took me to think it, but even at that I had the feeling I had been far too long figuring it out. I came down with the conviction that at any moment someone would be coming down that fire escape I was leaving uncovered and would be getting away from me.

Late to move, I could allow myself to lose no more time. I wheeled away from the window and took off on the run for the head of the alley. I think I took off. Maybe I did

make one step. Certainly I managed no more than that, and I'm not guaranteeing that I achieved even one.

Let's leave it that I had no more than turned away when it hit me. What hit me? I hate to tell you. Since nobody who died by a headman's ax or by the guillotine ever survived the blow even briefly, there's never been anyone to report what it felt like. It can, however, be imagined. The way I imagine it, it would feel exactly like what hit me.

And I haven't yet given you all of it. All of it boggles the imagination. It wasn't just the fall of the blade's cutting edge on the back of my neck. My guillotine seemed to be fitted with plumbing. Simultaneously with the blade effect, I was deluged by a warm shower.

This is not something I have reconstructed from coming out of it soaking wet and enveloped in a billowing mound of detergent suds. I clearly remember the shower hitting me and I remember that, as I went down and out, it was not in the dazzle of blinding light that seems to be the momentary prelude to the black of unconsciousness. I remember it well. I fell through a cloud of glittering bubbles and on into darkness.

Okay. It wasn't a guillotine and it wasn't the headman's ax. It was a galvanized iron pailful of sudsy warm water. In that very moment when I had turned away from the window, the thing had been flung at me full force. The rim of the pail had caught me across the back of the neck, affecting me exactly as a rabbit punch might have done; and, even as the pail hit, its foamy contents sloshed all over me.

How long I might have lain unconscious in the pool of suds before I would have come to on my own, I don't know. I didn't have to do it on my own. I had help. When I came out of it, I was in Dinah's kitchen and Dinah was ministering to me. With one hand she was rubbing ice

cubes over the back of my neck while with the other she was dashing ice water into my face.

As I stirred and opened my eyes, I was aware that someone was talking to me, but just at that time I wasn't registering on words or their meanings. That came gradually. When it did come, it seemed to be nothing that would require close attention.

Dinah was explaining her choice of methods. She wasn't apologizing for them. She was only explaining.

"You're soaking wet anyhow," she was saying. "So wetter won't make no never mind. You've had your wash. You can call this your rinse cycle. If you want to know, I'm damn sick of bodies up against my door. So last night it was a filthy-dirty one and this morning it's a new-washed clean one. Dirty or clean, I don't want any more."

"What happened?" I sputtered.

I was foaming at the mouth, but it was only part of my general condition. I was foaming all over. If my words were lacking in originality, I make no apology for them. The range of things available for a man to say in his first moment of regaining consciousness is limited. To my credit it wasn't: "Where am I?"

"You tell me what happened," Dinah said. "You knocked yourself out washing up, and you smell like a Saturday-night whorehouse."

A man took it up. I had to blink foam away from my eyes before I could see who he was. It was our waiter of the night before. He was more informative than Dinah.

"Looks like you got hit with a pailful of detergent suds," he said. "The pail got you from behind and knocked you cold. You've got a welt running straight across the back of your neck. It's sticking out so far you could hang stuff from it like on a picture molding."

"Who did it?" I asked, fighting myself up to a sitting position. "Did you see?"

"We saw the damn suds come seeping in under the door," Dinah said. "So we opened up and we found you. That's all we saw."

I had hoped for more, but I hadn't been expecting it, and it wasn't that I would have assumed that Dinah and her people would go on with the policy of seeing nothing and hearing nothing and knowing nothing. Unlike the stuff she'd been feeding us the night before, what she was saying now would have put no strain on anyone's credulity. It was a busy kitchen, and a restaurant kitchen operating under full pressure is a noisy place. I was hearing it—the clang and clatter of pots, the slamming of freezer and refrigerator doors, the chatter of a chef's knife against a chopping board, the sound of running water, plus a complex of other kitchen noises I couldn't separate out or identify.

Past all that and through a stout, securely closed door they could hardly have heard the clang of pail against pavement, especially as it might well have been only a minor clang since pail had obviously not struck pavement in unbroken trajectory. The splash of the suds would have been an even smaller sound, and a man dropping from the ground-floor window to the alley pavement would have made no big bang. Even leaving the alley in a pounding run he wouldn't have been heard through the closed door and over the kitchen din.

"The building across the alley," I said. "Ground-floor flat—do you know who lives there?"

Dinah laughed. It was a derisive bark without the first note of fun in it.

"Over there?" she said. "It's always someone new. They come and they go and mostly they're not there long enough for me even to get to know what they look like, particularly

since I'm a busy woman and I take no time for gawping across the alley. Today it's got to be someone new because I can't remember it's ever been anybody who washed, not ever before."

Dinah and the waiter were ministering to me. The kitchen help seemed to be going ahead with the luncheon preparations without permitting my interruption to affect them appreciably. A couple of busboys were hard at work mopping around me, soaking up and washing away the suds that had seeped in under the door and the fat puffs of foam that had been dragged into the kitchen with me.

To facilitate their task they had propped the kitchen door open. Since, once they'd had me over the threshold, they hadn't dragged me far, I was sitting in my suds just inside the doorway and I had an unimpeded view of the window across the alley. It was an open window. I tried to remember how it had been when Inspector Schmidt and I had been out in the alley focused on it and later when I'd been out there alone standing guard on it. Closed? Raised as it was now?

I couldn't remember. I wasn't prepared to witness to it with any certainty, but it did look different. I could think of nothing that could be different about that window unless it would be that it had been shut and it was now open. I had only just achieved that brilliant conclusion when I was transfixed by the sudden appearance of a man at the window.

I'd had it so firmly fixed in my mind that whoever might have been in the room behind that window would now be long gone that now I had to make a quick revision in my thinking. It made no sense that he should be making a belated getaway; but, sense or no sense, he was there and he wasn't going to escape me this time. I came charging up

out of my sudsy puddle and I was halfway out to the alley before recognition set in. I pulled back in mid-charge.

The man I'd been bent on nabbing was Chief of Homicide Inspector Schmidt. He was hanging out of the window and looking up and down the alley. Turning back from craning out to the street, he saw me. Even though it had taken me a couple of beats to dislodge my preconceptions before I recognized him, he was even slower to recognize me. It was not that he had never seen me dripping wet before, but previously it had always been under circumstances when it was to have been expected. Fresh out from under a shower or climbing out of a swimming pool—it had been situations like that. Even then I had never come at him in the shape of an ambulatory bubble bath.

"It's only detergent," I said.

A lesser man might have been even momentarily distracted by the foam. In his place I'm afraid I would have stopped to ask what detergent and whence, but not the inspector. His curiosity about my condition could wait. Inspector Schmidt never takes his eye off the ball.

"Get him?" he asked.

"No," I had to confess.

"But you saw him? You can recognize and identify?"

"Not even that."

If at that point he had eaten me out, it could have been nothing more than I was throwing at myself. Never had I felt more the incompetent fool. The inspector said nothing. It's not his way. What's done is done. It's no good lingering over it. There's still the job to do, and setbacks never discourage Inspector Schmidt. They whet his appetite for getting along with it.

He climbed the windowsill and dropped to the alley.

"Mind if I use your phone?" he asked Dinah.

"Booth with a pay phone up front," Dinah said. "But

that's only if you're calling long distance. If it's local, you can use my kitchen phone."

"It's local."

The inspector hit the phone. He dialed Precinct and got on to Wishes Leary.

"Tenement across the alley from Dinah's," he said. "The ground-floor rear—Blue was killed there. That's it. He was killed in the flat, and the body was heaved out of the window after it'd been lying around dead for a while inside. The thing about it is that since then the place hasn't been vacant. Someone was there just now. Maybe he got the idea from Dinah, the way last night she was washing away the evidence that wasn't there. This morning some character was in there washing away some blood that was there. Baggy and I surprised him at it, but he got away without our seeing him. He didn't get away by much, but he did get away. When I got inside, the places he'd been scrubbing up were still warm from the hot water he'd been using. I'll have the lab boys do a work-up and, of course, we'll need to interview all the neighbors for what that'll be worth. The interviews will be for your men." There was a brief pause while Leary was talking. Then the inspector took it up again. "Great," he said. "We'll be in the flat and, Wishes, if you have a man you can spare for just a little while, we'll need someone to run up to Baggy's place and bring him a complete set of dry clothes. He's walking around in a dripping cloud of detergent suds. So watch it. I won't answer for what he might do if anyone calls him Bubbles."

"Make it Bubblehead," I said.

The inspector was having none of that.

"Oh, come off it," he said. "He outmaneuvered us, and there was no way it could have been foreseen or prevented."

I gave up on the self-reproaches, and asked him what happened at his end.

"Nothing much," he said.

I'll leave it to you how much. He'd gone inside and knocked. He'd shouted through the door, identifying himself. Having no answer and hearing no sound or movement inside, he had gone to work on the lock.

"It's a lot better lock than they have at Norah's or Dan's or his mother's," the inspector said. "It took me a while to get it open. When I got in, it was like you heard me telling Wishes. Nobody there, and a freshly scrubbed up floor that was not only still wet but still warm."

"His mother's lock?" I asked.

"She didn't seem like anybody's mother," the inspector said, "but Wishes just told me. The boys have checked it out. Eddie Blue's legal name was Blau, son of Henrietta."

IX.

It was summer in New York. So everything I'd been wearing was lightweight, drip-dry stuff. Quick drying as those materials are, they are not so quick that when we pulled out of Dinah's kitchen I wasn't still conspicuously moist. I was not dripping anymore, and my coating of froth had been rinsed away; but, in addition to being damp, everything on me still stank of that perfumed detergent.

The inspector led the way to the flat across the alley. Wishes and his battalions were on the way as were the specialists out of Homicide, but both groups had a longer way to go. We were there ahead of them. The place was almost what I would have expected the natural habitat of an Eddie Blue would be.

I say almost because there was the area of floor that had been scrubbed. It was still wet even though, in the time since the inspector had first come upon it, the wet had cooled. There was also about a fifteen-inch length of iron pipe that looked glisteningly clean. We had there a picture that couldn't have been more easily read. What my assailant had been working on was what had been a bloodstained section of floor and the bloodsmeared weapon that had been employed for the bashing in of Eddie Blue's head.

The bit of floor and the length of pipe, however, were unique in these rooms the murdered man had occupied. If any other part of the place or any other object in it had ever been cleaned, it could hardly have been during Eddie

Blue's tenancy. Unless, furthermore, a whole string of previous tenants had been equally content to live in filth and
litter, Dinah had been mistaken about the frequent turno-
ver of tenancy. Even if a man worked at it, he couldn't get
a place that dirty in a day. Such encrustations of grime and
such accumulations of debris can be achieved only over a
period of weeks, possibly even of months.

Cigarette butts and empty beer cans lay everywhere, and
everywhere lay the evidence that in one department that
seemed to have mattered to him Henrietta Blau's son had
led the good life. The empty whiskey bottles were by no
means as numerous as the beer-can empties, but there were
enough of them and all with labels that indicated that Mr.
Blue had been in the habit of shopping around among the
costlier brands of bonded, hundred-proof bourbon and
twenty-year-old scotch.

He had even gone for alcoholic exotica. Among the
scotches I spotted some Glenlivets. If these were astonish-
ing finds, the empties with the French labels defied belief.
Framboise. Mirabelle. Kirsch. There was no discernible
pattern to what seemed to have been his tastes, unless it
was that his preference was for only those spirits that were
the strongest and the costliest.

Such an assemblage of bottles would have been extraordinary anywhere. In those rooms with the roaches
crawling about in the empties they had me goggle-eyed. I
found myself doing mental arithmetic on how many
Mothers' Day ripoffs it might have taken to support this
kind of habit.

Amid all the junk on the floor, one particularly fancy
bottle caught my eye. Nothing could have been less important, but I was curious. I poked it with the toe of my shoe,
idly rolling it over to bring its label up into view. I'll never
know whether the label did come up or not. The bottle

rolled, and something far more arresting grabbed my attention. I lost all interest in labels, no matter how extraordinary.

It was a bright yellow, metallic glint. I was telling myself it would be nothing but a bit of gold-colored foil. You'll find the stuff sealed around the necks of pretentious bottles. It's a luxury look that's added in the hope of justifying the staggering price. When I'd stooped for a closer look, however, I called the inspector over.

It wasn't foil. It was solid. It was chunky. My first thought about it was that it might be evidence that the late Black and Blue in his mugging operations had not made an exclusive specialty of ripping off the welfare mothers. It was a cuff link and of the heavy, angular kind that for some time had been fashionable along Madison Avenue. Do your lunchtime drinking at one of the right bars in the East Fifties and you'll see the account executives. They show the proper inch of shirt cuff each time they lift a martini and in that proper inch will flash this sort of cuff link. I've often wondered about the strength it must take to hoist a four-ounce martini when a man is hoisting with it such a weight of eighteen-carat gold. I could never believe that it needed all that metal just to hold two ends of a shirt cuff together. Such links could be used for coupling railway cars.

Despite all those expensive bottles, no one even for a moment could think that the cuff link might have belonged to Eddie Blue. Anyone who'd ever seen the man or his remains would have to say, "No way."

Cuff links were just not his style and that would have gone for any cuff links. Undershirts were his style, or T-shirts. A man who doesn't have cuffs doesn't use cuff links. I had to think that any gold cuff link we found in Eddie Blue's place could be nothing but part of the loot from some mugging he'd pulled off. It could be his only in the

sense that he had been holding it after he had taken illegal possession of it and until he might get around to fencing it.

The inspector picked it up. Lying on his open palm it seemed even more impressive.

"I guess he hit men as well as women," I said. "This can't be anything but loot."

"Loot like this," the inspector said, "he would have fenced. Until he got around to fencing it, he wouldn't have left it kicking around on the floor. He'd have taken better care of it."

"He's pulled a job. He brings the loot home. He's going to stow it somewhere until he gets around to fencing it. He drops this cuff link and loses it in the trash he has all over the floor."

"And he just leaves it there? Easy come, easy go?"

"He was killed. Maybe it was a fight over the division of the loot. Maybe they were struggling over the stuff, grabbing at it, fighting each other for it. This dropped to the floor. The fight went on. Blue was killed. No time after that to hang about looking for a cuff link."

"Time to come back and wash up blood," the inspector said.

"That was the most pressing task. After that he was going to search for the cuff link maybe, but there wasn't any after that. You came along and messed up his schedule."

"It's monogrammed," the inspector said.

Tilting his palm, he made the thing roll toward me. The monogrammed side of it came up into view. Actually, seen from that angle, the thing was virtually all monogram. It was two massive gold letters rising in high relief from a heavy gold base. The letters were DM.

"If they were EB," I said, "I couldn't for a minute think they were Blau's. So now the same thing goes for DM and Dan Mallard. People without cuffs don't wear cuff links."

"Who then?"

I shrugged.

"What's Dinah's surname?" I asked.

I knew better than that, but I was using it for filler while I was trying to make sense of Dan Mallard.

"Brooks," Schmitty answered, "and she's the wrong sex."

"I don't know. Aren't these the unisex days? Also how about Dennis the Menace?"

"DM," the inspector said. "What about Dead Man?"

"Makes as good sense as Mallard. If you'll let me repeat, people without cuffs . . . "

"I don't know that it'll hold up. Every time we've seen him it's true that he hasn't been wearing anything that would take cuff links. It's hard to imagine him wearing them of his own accord."

"That's for sure, but it's also hard to imagine him coerced into cuff links."

"In his business it could be easy. If his sponsors go for the massive fist wielding the diaper pin, why not the massive fist in the fancy, turnback cuff? I can see it and I can hear the spiel: 'Dress like the line-backers dress when the line-backers aren't backing line.' They'd buy that in Peoria."

"Yes," I said. That much I was ready to concede. "As costume, before the cameras, it would be more than possible. But coming over here in costume? Coming over in costume to scrub the floor? Rolling back the french cuffs so he can do the scrubbing and losing a cuff link in the process?"

"Certainly not then," the inspector said. "When we came over here now, we'd only just left Mallard. He could no more than barely have made it over here before we got to the alley. He could have done the scrubbing while we were out in the alley, but he couldn't possibly have found the

time to change his shirt before he came over, and he would never have changed into something more formal than that T-shirt we saw him in, not for scrubbing a floor."

"Last night," I scoffed. "He brought the Simms kids to Dinah's back room for dinner. While he was in the neighborhood, he slipped across the alley to knock Blue's head in. It was then he lost the cuff link because, after all, he couldn't have taken the kids to Dinah's back room without dressing for dinner. Black tie at the least. Kids are impressionable. A man has to set a good example."

The inspector wasn't amused.

"There are other possibilities," he said.

"Someone who has keys," I suggested. "We know he has a key or keys to Norah's door and to Mallard's door. Why not a key to this place as well?"

"If we assume that it wasn't Danny Boy himself who locked us in last night—Mallard or Norah. We have only their word for it that her door was also locked from the outside."

"Right." I had to accept this other possibility. "But making the assumption," I continued, "it could have been a burglary of Mallard's place—the cuff links and whatever else stolen out of there."

By this time our reinforcements were arriving. The inspector took it up with Wishes.

"Mallard went on and on about crime in their building," he said. "He fed it to us in what seemed like complete detail. He made no mention of burglary, not of his place or of any of the other flats. He also made no mention of his ever having been mugged. Did you at any time have a report over at Precinct?"

"Never," Wishes said, "but then not everything gets reported. You know that."

"I can't believe the cuff link is his," I said.

Leary backed me up.

"Mallard?" he said. "No way. The initials have to be a coincidence. The day you catch him in cuff links you can look to catch me in a brassiere. That's how much use he'd have for them ever."

"Making it all the more likely that he could lose one and never know it was missing," the inspector said.

"He'd have to have been wearing it first if he was going to lose it," I argued.

The inspector did some thinking aloud. He had earlier suggested the possibility of costume for one of Mallard's TV commercials. He brought that up again.

"Obviously if he came over here last night, it wasn't in costume," he said. "Even more he didn't this morning because this morning we know it's a matter of couldn't as well as of wouldn't. We're still left with the possibility that he did stop by here some other time. It may even have been many other times. Let's say it might have been on his way home from doing a dress-up commercial. He stopped by here to see Blue about something. He lost the cuff link here. He went on home and made the quickest possible change. Tearing out of the clothes he couldn't be comfortable in, he wouldn't be giving them enough attention to notice he was minus a cuff link."

Wishes took it up.

"All previous muggings in that building were two-man jobs," he said. "Norah's yesterday was a one-man deal. Mallard the other man? Then it would have been the one-man deal yesterday because Mallard would never hit Norah. He's crazy about her. He talks a lot about not liking to be middle class, but there's SoHo, there's communes, there's the Village. He doesn't have to live in that lousy tenement. It's only because of her."

"When he first talked to Schmitty and me," I said, "he

made a great point of how Norah's mugging was different. He made more of the two-man deal it had always previously been than she did herself. Why would he have gone on and on about it if he had always been the second man?"

"TV," the inspector said. "The most obvious suspect is never the guilty man."

"More than that," Leary said. "If Norah has any suspicions, Mallard would be in there early and often to convince her that, no matter what she might have known or suspected about the other muggings, in this one he had no part."

At that point Inspector Schmidt came up with a new idea.

"We keep talking about two-man jobs," he said. "How about two-person jobs? How about just the mother-and-son team using her flat as a base? I think we can assume they did use her flat that way. It explains why you never got anywhere with your stakeouts over there, Wishes. Ma Blau had a grandstand seat for every move you made in the building. Also it was great for getaways. Ripoff in the hall and no need to go running out of the building. He just goes to earth in Mom's place. We have to keep that possibility open, too. There may never have been a second man—just a second person, Henrietta Blau."

Captain Leary liked it.

"Then Blue is killed in retaliation for what he did to Norah, and Blau is killed because she was in it, too."

For me, it wouldn't quite jell.

"But she wasn't in on this one," I reminded them. "We've had that most emphatically. This was the solo effort."

"Suppose we try breaking that down," the inspector said. "Our authority for that is only Norah Simms. We had it

from both Norah and Mallard, but taking it this way, Mallard wouldn't know anything but what Norah told him. So Norah knows who did it to her, and she's not settling for anything short of taking the law into her own hands. She's going to get even. An eye for an eye, a tooth for a tooth. Two lives for a fetus? Why not? She knows what she's set on doing, but she's not going to make it easy for us to catch up with her after she's done it. She says she was mugged by only one man. We are to be faced with two connected murders. Maybe we'll look in other directions. These killings can't have anything to do with her. She was ripped off by only one person, not two. If anybody's getting even, maybe it'll look like one of the other women in the building, one of the victims of the two-people job."

"She's going to get her own revenge?" Leary said. "Why did Mallard go to you then?"

"She didn't send him. He went on his own, and he didn't come to me. He sounded off to Baggy, and then he was trapped. Baggy brought him to me. Since he fed me the story, she'd fed him, there was no harm done. It could have been that, even before anybody was killed, we were being maneuvered so we'd look away from her when we came to deal with the killings."

It was about this time that the man Captain Leary had sent up to my place returned with my complete change of clothes. Inspector Schmidt took me over to the precinct station house to do my switch. He was setting himself up a command post in Leary's office.

As soon as I'd started stripping down, I knew that I needed more than the change of clothes. The detergent had soaked through everything. It was in my hair. I could smell it on my skin.

I suppose if I'd had to I could have lived with it for the rest of the day; but since there were showers in the station-

house basement, I allowed myself the luxury of washing the stink out of my hair and sluicing it off my body. It took longer under the shower than you might think before I stopped frothing and was rid of the smell.

I had returned to the captain's office and was climbing into my fresh clothes when the desk sergeant rang through. He had an informant call he thought Inspector Schmidt would want to take. There was an extension phone I could pick up. The inspector suggested that I listen in with him.

The caller was a woman. She was not going to identify herself. If the inspector wanted to hear what she had to say, he could listen. That, however, was to be the whole of it. She was telling what she knew. She was telling it this once and only this once. She was not going to be available to give testimony. She was not going to make any signed statements. She wasn't crazy. She knew the score, and she was one gal who wasn't ready to die. Not by a long shot, she wasn't.

"They've killed two," she said. "They won't stop at a third. If they knew I was talking, my life wouldn't be worth two cents."

"They?" the inspector said. "Who are they?"

"Them two—the Simms bitch and her actor boyfriend."

"Norah Simms?"

"Yeah. Her."

"And Dan Mallard?"

"Yeah. And him."

"Two killings?"

I knew what the inspector was doing. He was pulling the thing out, doing what he could to make it last. It takes time for the phone company to come through with an identification on the phone from which a call is being made. Once the caller has hung up, there isn't a chance.

I didn't know whether or not he'd want the caller

nabbed, but it was obvious that he wanted her identified. Anonymous informants are a nuisance. All too frequently they are cranks who know nothing. Knowing who they are can be a great help toward evaluating what they have to tell you.

"Yeah, two. Old lady Blau and that fighter guy earlier."

"What's the connection between those two?"

"They both of them seen too much. They both of them knew too much."

"What makes you say that?"

"Him—this guy Blue—he was always in and out of the old lady's place. Anybody they got mugged, it was always right outside her door."

She went into details. The Mothers' Day routine had always been grabbing the victim as she came into the building and dragging her to the rear of the ground-floor hall where under the stairs it was always the darkest.

"It was never no place without it was like right outside her door. She could see through her keyhole."

The crank flavor was growing strong. Lines of sight available through a keyhole are narrowly limited. Even if the peeper is peering into a brightly lighted area, he is not likely to see much of anything unless what he is looking at is directly in line of sight and sufficiently static to afford him time for recognition.

A mugging is never such an event. It's an act of violence. The participants don't stand frozen in one attitude long enough for anyone looking through a keyhole to make anything of them. Such a scene viewed through a keyhole is never going to be anything more than a blur.

The rest of what his informant fed the inspector seemed to be just as reliable. It was theory masquerading as fact, and even as theory I couldn't see it to be worth much. The work of an amateur theorist and one who, judging from her

language, was hardly dispassionate and objective in the formation of her hypothesis.

The voice dripped malice. There was no need for anyone to work at keeping her going. She went on and on. What she was trying to tell seemed to be growing in the telling. I had the impression that she had called on impulse with only the most general notion of the charges she was going to lay against Norah Simms and Dan Mallard. If one thing appeared to lead to another in her telling, her accusations seemed to be forming themselves in just that way. Her own words, as she heard herself speak them, brought to her mind further accusations and further arguments. As each fresh idea popped into her head, she put it into words without ever stopping to think about what she was saying.

Blau and Blue were dead because they had been keyhole witnesses to all the violent acts that had been perpetrated in the dark behind the stairs. Without ever having seen anything, however, all the rest of the people in the house knew. Nothing could be plainer. Every welfare mother in the building had been hit and not only once each. To some of them it had happened twice and to some even oftener.

"All of them but her," the woman said. "Every last one but her. People got to talking. Who's so dumb they didn't begin to dig what was going on? So yesterday's the big deal. She's the one gets hit except with her it's got to be different."

The difference referred to was in the number of muggers. Two working together all the other times shrank to only one when Norah Simms was hit.

"You know why?"

The inspector wasn't required to say whether he knew or not. The flood swept on full spate. The why of it, granted its premises, was indisputably logical. It had always been the two of them working together. If, however, they were

staging a fake mugging just to stop the talk and to knock off the mounting suspicion, it had to be only one doing the mugging. After all, it was the other one this time being mugged.

"They had to tell everybody it was different that way because they had a hunch the old bitch Blau and her boyfriend could've been seeing something and maybe, without seeing any more, they'd seen how it was different this time."

Obviously the information we had—that Eddie Blue was Henrietta Blau's son—hadn't gotten around, but I knew what the dame meant. There was no difficulty over that. The way she had it, Norah and Dan could have skipped telling people that Norah's mugging had been different. They had hoped that anything Blau and Blue might have seen would be covered by the story the two miscreants were peddling, but that had been a vain hope. The Blau-Blue combo had seen too much. With what they'd seen they had attempted blackmail.

"That one, even old as she was, she'd do anything for money."

The inspector knew what the blackmail attempt had gotten Blau and Blue, and his informant broke off to kick around the thought that she might be crazy to be talking to him. She decided, however, that having gone this far, she might just as well tell him everything. Everything meant steadily fancier theorizing.

It also included one startling item which also could have come, as the rest of it seemed to have done, completely out of her head. She did, however, cite a definite source for this one bit. She knew this because it had been told to her by both Norah Simms and Dan Mallard. They were getting married. It was going to be quick, as quick as possible—only the required wait for the blood tests.

"How do you like that?" The babe was beside herself with gleeful malice. She obviously didn't know whether she wanted to be puritanically disapproving or obscenely hilarious. "How do you like that?" she repeated. "All this time she's been playing around with Mallard, but only playing around. For the shacking up, there's been some other guy. Some other guy, he keeps her knocked up all the time and all the time having his babies. So now she's making the switch to Mallard and it's going to be legal even. They've got to fix it somehow they'll knock off all the talk it's going around about the two of them. What's making folks say it's them been ripping off all the mothers? It's just she's the only one . . . she's never been ripped off. So it's got to be her this once and they got to make it look good."

With her gift for words, our voluble informant called it killing two birds with one stone.

"All them kids. They was coming along always like one was chasing another out of her belly, and they'd been coming way before anybody's even seen Mallard. So they ain't his, not any of them. They all of them look alike and they don't look like her and they don't look like Mallard. So now she's making the switch. She's getting married and all. Are they going to want to do it with another of this other guy's kids on the way? So it's them two birds with the one rock. She gets hit so bad she loses the baby. That's just the kind of thing they need to make it look good, like it's the real thing, like it's as bad as anybody else got it, that and worse. But it's the kid he don't want her to have. So they get rid of it."

"This other man," the inspector asked, "the guy she's quitting for Mallard? Do you know him?"

"How would I know him?"

"You know so many things."

He made it sound like flattery.

"I ain't nobody's dope," she said. "But me, I minds my own business. I don't go spying on nobody or keeping tabs on nobody. Johns, they're coming in and going upstairs all the time. Sometimes I see them go by. Sometimes I don't. I don't sit in my window watching all the time. I don't peep through my keyhole or crack in my door to see who goes where once he's come into the house. Maybe I seen him. Maybe I ain't. I don't know."

You may have noticed that by this time she was so carried away with what she was telling that she had let slip more than enough information about herself. Any time the inspector might want her, he would have a shrewd idea of where he could go to find her. She saw men go into the building and go upstairs. It was my guess that she would have to be the tenant in the ground-floor front, living under Norah Simms as Henrietta Blau had lived under Dan Mallard.

For someone who didn't peep and didn't watch, she knew a great deal or at least she professed to much knowledge. It was her belief that Norah Simms didn't have men up in her flat. Considering how overrun with small boys her rooms were, I could well understand how Norah might have considered it necessary to go to her man instead of having him come to her. There was also the welfare mother's need for keeping away from the welfare people's notice any man who might be in regular attendance.

This informant, however, would allow Norah Simms neither such small degree of delicacy nor any modicum of practical good sense.

"She's got to be better than anybody else," she said. These words she was spitting into the telephone. It seemed to me that she had worked herself up to the summit of her malice. From her tone, you could have thought she had now come around to telling the inspector the worst she had

to say about Norah Simms and Dan Mallard. "She goes off someplace to get herself laid. Maybe that way she thinks everybody'll get the idea she don't get hers like anybody else. We'll think maybe the stork brings them. Well, I ain't never seen no stork flying in her window. She can go running around any time she like⌐. She's got that Mallard baby-sitting for her all the time and now she's marrying him. How do you like that? What kind of a man holds still for the way she's been doing him? I'll tell you what kind. It's a guy he's pimping for her, and it's a guy she's got so much on him he's got to marry her to keep her quiet. A wife can't testify against her husband. That's what. You mark my words. That's what."

There was a lot more of it, but I've given you everything that could have been of any consequence. The rest was a lot of stuff about how Norah Simms thought she was better than anyone else. She carried her nose in the air. She treated people as though to her they smelled bad, and the inspector's informant wanted him to know that Norah Simms didn't smell any different.

On the subject of Mallard, she appeared unable to choose between questioning his virility and denying his masculinity. When she wasn't characterizing his behavior as that of a pimp, she was calling him a fag and hinting that it was only the purposes of a pederast that had him spending so much of his time riding herd on the Simms kids.

When at last she rang off, the desk sergeant was ready to fill the inspector in on the lady. She had been on the line more than long enough for the phone company to come up with the location of the telephone she was using. It was a street-corner booth. A patrol car, alerted to drive by and check it, had come through with immediate identification.

It had been easy. She was a neighborhood character.

Every officer in the precinct would recognize her on sight. In a neighborhood that abounded in prostitutes, she was the most conspicuous of the lot.

"Her name's Hazel, Inspector," the desk sergeant said. "I don't remember the rest of it, but everybody knows her. I can't figure what's eating her. You can never get anything out of that one and now to go on and on the way she done."

"When we go around to the ground-floor front and try to question her," the inspector said, "she'll revert to type quick enough. She'll know nothing and she'll have nothing to tell us."

The desk sergeant blinked.

"You got her ID out of her while I was handling another call?" he asked.

"She didn't know what she was doing," the inspector said. "She handed it to me."

"Yeah," the sergeant said. "If I can say it, Inspector, it's the only thing she handed you. That one, you can never believe a word she says. We get crank calls all the time, but hers was a beaut."

I was inclined to agree with him. Running her whole harangue through a mental filter to isolate from it any residue of fact, I found myself left with only the one item: Norah Simms was about to marry Dan Mallard, and even that could be true or not true. Inspector Schmidt was inclined to agree with me but not all the way.

"Let's not be too quick to discount her," he said. "Of course, it's not anything like testimony. It's all conjecture or, at least, almost all, but there may be a kind of folk wisdom in it. It looks to me like she's got it ass-backwards, but I won't guarantee that she hasn't got something."

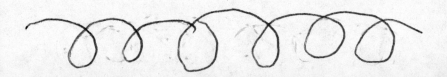

X.

If she did have anything, none of it was forthcoming in face-to-face confrontation. The inspector had talked to her before. After the Henrietta Blau murder, he had left most of the neighbors to Leary's men; but since her place had been the closest to the murdered woman's ground-floor rear, he had taken her himself. He'd had nothing from her then but complaints about the uproar, and you know what that was. It was our uproar.

So now again, as was to have been expected, he got nothing from her. The boys in the prowl car who had seen her in the street-corner booth were mistaken. If they weren't simply lying, then it had to be that they had seen what they wanted to see. It was nothing new. It was the story of her life.

The streets seethed with crime. Muggers and rapists lurked in every corner, not to speak of the animals from whom a girl could fear both mugging and rape.

"Do the cops ever touch them? You can bet your life they don't. They're too busy giving me a hard time."

To hear her tell it, her life was just one frame after another. Although she did believe herself to be as pretty as a picture, there was no reason for it. She was always under totally unmerited police harassment and this was more of the same.

"Me in a phone booth?" she said. "Where would I get the dime?"

When the inspector fed back to her what she had observed and what she had failed to observe, all that nonsense about her keyhole and the crack in her door, she met his evidence by broadening the base of her complaint. It wasn't only the police she had on her back. It was everyone.

"People know how it is with the cops having it in for me. People know that, whatever goes around here, first thing you've got the whole damn force working to pin it on little Hazel. Any bitch, she wants to pull something, she makes it look like it was me done it. It's the easy way. They're not going to be looking for nobody else."

What made the inspector think she would be stupid enough to make a call like that and then give herself away the way the inspector was saying she had done? Nobody was that stupid.

"A call like what?" Inspector Schmidt asked her.

The woman was stupid, but not so stupid that the question didn't alert her to the fact that she had just made another slip. He'd said nothing about the content of the call, only that he wanted to go over with her the information she had given in her call to Precinct.

"Like what?" she said. "Like a call to the station house. Like giving information. Like that, mister."

It was no good. She was stonewalling, and that's a technique that requires no skill, no quick thinking, nothing in the way of nimble wit. It takes nothing but brazen effrontery and, whatever Hazel might have lacked in other departments, the brass was there and in abundance.

Dropping all talk of the call, the inspector tried taking it from scratch. She came up with none of the stuff she had been feeding him over the phone. She knew nothing. She had no opinions.

It wasn't until he had given up on her and we were starting upstairs that she opened up at all. She followed us out to the hall and, when she saw the way we were headed, she was suddenly helpful.

"If you're going up there to look for the lovebirds," she said, "they ain't home, neither of them."

"The lovebirds?"

The inspector was deadpanning it.

"Yeah, them. Ain't you heard? Wedding bells, orange blossoms."

She hummed a couple bars of the *Lohengrin* wedding march. For a rendition like that, Richard Wagner would have cut her throat.

"Who?" the inspector asked.

"Norah and Danny," she said. "Who else? They been going steady. You must have noticed."

"I noticed she's got a houseful of kids and they're none of them his."

"So what? He's a good man, that Danny. He'll make them a good father. He's like a father to them already. Plenty of fathers, they should only be so good to their kids and their wives, too. They should only be half as good to their wives. He'll make her a good husband."

"A sudden switch for her, isn't it?"

If the inspector had hoped to elicit a repeat on the wife-can't-testify-against-her-husband insinuation, Hazel wasn't falling into that trap.

She shrugged.

"That Women's Lib crap," she said. "She went for that. She was taking care of herself and she was taking care of her kids. She didn't need no man to lean on and she didn't need no man to protect her. So yesterday she learned different. She can use a man to protect her, and she's got a man hanging around her with all them muscles on him. All

she needed was to find out she needed him. So she found out."

"How do you know they're getting married?"

"He told me. He told everybody. He was dancing up and down the stairs, jumping like a kid, shaking the whole house. She kept trying to shush him, but she said, yes, they was going to do it. That's where they went, to see about the license, to get the blood tests." She snickered for just a moment and a touch of malice slipped past her mask of generosity. "They got all the kids with them," she said. "You know, like to give the bride away."

Her little joke seemed to grow on her. What had begun as a snicker exploded into a guffaw.

Working up through the building, the inspector had from the other tenants only more of the same. An exuberant Dan Mallard had pranced about, proclaiming his joy. Norah Simms, it appeared, had been echoing him, but in a far more subdued fashion. A realist in one of the flats in the upper reaches of the building commented on the contrast in their moods.

"He's the happy one," she said, "and what's he got to be so happy about, taking on all them mouths to feed and none of them his?"

"She isn't happy?" the inspector asked.

"Not like him, she ain't. Not like she had ought to be."

"Like him," however, might have taken a bit of doing, because it was just then that Mallard came home and he was making no secret of his arrival. His tread on the stairs was thunderous but, in comparison with the full-lunged bellow of his singing, it seemed like nothing much. In terms of the legally required waiting period which would make marriage in the morning a few days soon, his song might have been ill chosen, but only in those terms. He was singing "Get Me to the Church on Time."

Although we heard no one but Mallard, I assumed Norah would be with him. She didn't have the weight it would take to shake the stairs the way he did or the chest capacity for filling the air with such stentorian din. She and the whole troop of small boys could have been joining him in song and there would be no knowing it. Any other voices would have been drowned out by his gargantuan roar.

By the time we had trotted down three flights of stairs, he was in Norah's place with the door shut behind him. Even a good, stout door would have done little to make him less audible, and these doors were anything but stout.

The inspector knocked, but that was just for the record. There wasn't a chance Mallard would hear the knock. We pounded, but even that he didn't hear. The inspector tried the door. Mallard hadn't locked it. We went in and found him as might have been expected, doing a spectacularly rhythmic job of diapering his small namesake, keeping the process in time with his singing.

Showing no surprise at our appearance, he welcomed us with a fresh outburst of joy. If the thought so much as entered his head that we might have come with any purpose other than offering him our congratulations, he was giving not the smallest sign of it. He was a happy man. He expected all the world to participate in his happiness. He had all the Simms boys around him. They were giving every appearance of participating, or perhaps they were just entranced with his singing. Small boys like large noises.

"Wedding breakfast in Dinah's back room," he shouted. "You've got to be there—the blast of the century. Dinah's already made a start on laying the foundations for the cake she's building us."

I congratulated him.

"I hope we're not going to spoil it," the inspector said.

"Nothing can spoil it." Mallard was suddenly sobered.

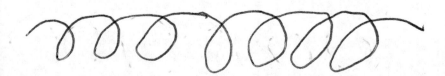

"Nothing. Nobody. A million times it's been no, and now finally it's yes."

It sounded more like an incantation than a statement.

"Where's the lucky woman?" the inspector asked.

"Out."

"That much we can see. Out where?"

"I've never asked her to give me accountings. I'm not asking her now and I won't even after we're married. Love and trust and no questions asked."

"I'm different. I'm not marrying her."

"Damn right, you're not. No way."

"Then she's not here for questions, but you are. What have you been doing since we saw you last?"

"Asking her for the millionth and somethingth time. Getting knocked over by her saying yes. Getting up off the floor, but way up to where I'm walking on air, and that's where I've been ever since—walking on air."

"And where have you done all this walking—chronologically and in full detail."

Mallard looked at the inspector hard and from the inspector to me. He broke out in a broad grin.

"What's eating on you now?" he asked. "Somebody been locking you up again?"

"We ask the questions," the inspector told him.

"You sure enough do," Mallard said, "but today you've caught me in a great mood. Today I don't mind anything. So here goes."

If Inspector Schmidt wanted complete detail, he got it and running over. Our session with Norah and him earlier that morning had upset her. She had wanted to be alone for a while. So it had seemed a good time to go off to do his daily jogging.

"That's business," he explained. "It's one of the things I have to do to keep the muscles pretty."

"Immediately after we left you?"

"Practically on your heels."

After he had returned from his jogging and had washed up and changed out of his sweaty T-shirt, he had gone next door to Norah's flat to talk about the pilot he was to make with little Danny and about the possibilities of TV work for all the kids.

"We were talking about it," he said, "and it hit me how I had a new angle for asking her. The kids get into the commercials racket. They make a bundle. She can't go on saying she won't burden me with another guy's children. The troops will be pulling down their own bread. So if it was money bothering her, now it'll be just the two of us and the kids we'll be having together. These will be just for loving, not for supporting."

"Has she told you she's planning on having her tubes tied off?"

The question rocked Mallard. Moments passed before he was able to speak at all, and then his words were a mumble of anger and disgust.

"She told me, but, goddammit, she didn't tell you. You get into everything, don't you? It could be you'll make me vomit."

I wanted to tell him the inspector wasn't into this for kicks, but Schmitty had the man off base and I knew he wanted to keep him there. I said nothing.

"You expect to change her mind?" the inspector asked.

"Not that it's any of your business, but just to shut you up, she has changed her mind. She wasn't going to have another and lose it like the one yesterday, but there won't be any more of that. We're moving out of here. We'll have a decent place to live and she won't be making any more Mothers' Day trips."

"Running out on your own kind of people?"

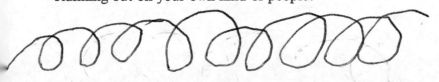

Schmitty was taunting him with his own words.

"Taking my kind of people with me," Mallard answered. He indicated the Simms boys. "Now they're going to be more than that. They'll be my own."

"Then that's okay. What are you going to wear to be married in?"

Mallard laughed. He was too full of joy to hold anger long.

"What's wrong with these?" he asked, indicating what he had on—blue jeans and a white T-shirt.

"Striped pants and a morning coat might be too much of a switch," the inspector said.

"Striped pants and a morning coat would scare Norah off. She wouldn't know it was me."

"Then you won't be needing this."

The inspector opened his hand and displayed the cuff link.

"That I never needed," Mallard began. He stopped short. He was thinking. "Hey," he said. "What goes on? Where did you get it?"

"Where did you lose it?"

"I didn't or maybe I did. How the hell would I know?"

"It is yours?"

"DM— Daniel Mallard. A grateful sponsor gave them to me when beer sales went through the roof. It was a German beer company. Maybe they thought it would change the way I dress. So far as I'm concerned the DM stands for *Deutschmark*. I never wore them."

"What did you do with them?"

"Nothing. I dumped them in a drawer along with a lot of other junk sponsors have given me. Ask me what's all in there, and I couldn't tell you. Useless junk—I forget I've got it."

"They come in pairs," the inspector said. "Where's the other one?"

Mallard shrugged.

"You tell me," he said. "Maybe it's where this one was when I last saw them. Maybe it's where you found this one. I wouldn't know."

"Let's go look," the inspector suggested.

"Let's," Mallard agreed. "One's not much good without the other unless a man's planning on losing an arm. Even together they're no good to me. You might as well have the pair if you want them."

He picked up the baby and lined up the other kids. We moved it next door to his place. The moment he swung the door open, I smelled it. It was a smell I would have known anywhere, a smell I don't expect I'll ever forget. He smelled it too. Stopping in the doorway, he wrinkled his nose.

"What the hell's that?" he said.

The inspector pushed past him. What it was couldn't have been more obvious. The smell emanated from a corner of the room. Lying on the floor in a small heap, there were some wet clothes that smelled pretty much as I had smelled before I showered and changed. When we went inside and came up close to them, I recognized that it was even worse. They smelled just as I had smelled before Dinah had put me through what she'd called my rinse cycle.

Picking up the reeking garments, the inspector offered them for Mallard's inspection. There were a pair of sandals and a pair of blue jeans. Those were duplicates of what Mallard was wearing except that the ones he had on were not wet and not reeking of that nauseously perfumed detergent.

"These yours?" the inspector asked.

Mallard examined them. He was saying nothing. He was

being slow and careful. He went to his closet and checked its contents.

"They're mine or they're exactly like some of mine that are missing," he said. "I don't know which. When I last went out of here, sandals and jeans just like these were in the closet. They were dry and they didn't stink of anything unless it was me. What the hell is this all about? Don't I get to know?"

"When I find out, I'll tell you. That is, if you really have to wait that long."

"If that means you think I know and I should be telling you," Mallard said, "forget it. I don't understand any of it. It's crazy."

There was one garment more. It was also wet and reeking of the perfumed detergent. Up to this point the inspector had been leaving it where it lay, but that doesn't mean anybody was ignoring it. It was a white shirt. It was obviously a cheap, bargain-basement job, but it was fancy. It had french cuffs and the way it lay on the floor, both cuffs were visible. Neither one was fastened. One showed empty buttonholes. From the other dangled the mate to the DM cuff link Dan Mallard said he had never worn.

The inspector indicated the shirt.

"And this?" he asked.

Mallard scowled.

"You can see that the cuff link is the mate," he said, "so you can't be asking about that. The shirt? Not mine. I've never had one like it. I never wear anything like it. How it got here, I don't know. Why it's here, I also don't know. Obviously you are finding it meaningful. I am not, so until you fill me in . . ."

"Never's a lot of time. Try to remember. What about costume? Never played a dress-up part?"

Mallard didn't take even a moment for thinking about it

or for trying to remember. His reply was quick and une-
quivocal.

"Dress-up parts," he said. "You don't know TV, brother.
They get you typed before you're even given a start and,
once you're typed, you stay typed. All the way I've been
typed for beefcake. If there are sleeves, they have to be
short enough to show the biceps, but mostly there are no
sleeves because there is no shirt. The pectorals have to be
on view. The pectorals play a big part in making Dan Mallard valuable merchandise."

Inspector Schmidt worked at it. He visualized a commercial in which Big Dan would come on dressed to the nines.
Slowly he'd roll up his sleeves to reveal the biceps or he'd
peel off the shirt to put the pectorals on display.

"Like that," Schmitty said, "it might be the big effect.
You know, promise, suspense, strip-tease stuff, all the
drama of an unveiling."

Mallard looked sick, but he rallied for what I'm certain
he intended for an insult.

"You're in the wrong job, Inspector," he said. "Switch to
advertising. You could end up in the next Nixon White
House."

"You never did a job where they used you that way?"

"Never. They're selling the product. They aren't selling
me."

So there it stood when Norah's homecoming provided an
interruption. When we'd first come into his place and been
assaulted by that sickening perfume, Mallard had rushed to
the windows and thrown them wide and, when I had shut
the door behind us, he'd come around back of me to set it
ajar. He was trying to air the stench out of the place.

When Norah came along, therefore, she caught it while
she was still out in the hall. From out there, she couldn't
see either the inspector or me. So far as she could have

known, Mallard was alone in there with her brood. She was talking to him before she came through the door into his flat.

She was telling him that from here on out, she would do the washing and the cleaning and that, if he ever wanted to help, it was going to have to be only under her orders and her direction.

"I thought you knew your way around this kind of stuff," she said as she came through the door, "but whatever got into you to use this stinking junk? You don't even have to open the package. You can get the smell right through the sealed box. It's going to be weeks before you'll get it out of here."

Mallard grabbed her and kissed her.

"Not us, my darling," he said. "The next tenant. We won't be here."

I had expected that she would push him off. She had never seemed the type to care for exhibitionist displays. I couldn't imagine that she would ever be happy about letting strangers into her private life. The descriptions we'd had of Mallard's exuberance and the contrast of her subdued mien seemed more natural to her than the show she was now putting on for us. She clung to him and she covered his face with kisses. She was climbing all over him.

It was startling and not only to the inspector and me. Anyone could have seen that it had caught Mallard off base. For a moment he was so much taken aback that the only reaction he seemed able to find to the violence of her passionate display was an oafishly awkward astonishment. It didn't take him long, however, to rise to the occasion and switch over to simple enjoyment.

Eventually she came up for breath, and he grinned at us. If he was remembering anything of the cuff links or the shirt, he could have been setting it aside for thinking about

at some other time. His demeanor was saying, "First things first." He came close to putting it into words.

"Look, fellows," he said. "Couldn't you just go away and come back later. You can be spoiling something beautiful."

"Sorry," the inspector said. "A few questions for the bride."

She turned to us to indicate that she was ready for the questions, but in turning she didn't pull away from Mallard. Standing close up against him, she drew his arm around her. Evidently she wanted him holding her close while she would be questioned, and obviously that was the kind of duty he liked.

The inspector began with no more than the amenities.

"We've already congratulated the bridegroom. We'd like to wish you luck."

"Thank you," she said. "I have it."

"I hope I won't need to interfere with it," the inspector told her.

"Nothing can interfere with it," she said.

"That's telling him, baby," Mallard said, but the look of worried confusion, temporarily erased by her shower of kisses, was creeping back into his eyes.

The inspector picked up the detergent-soaked shirt.

"Recognize this?"

She took it from his hand and inspected it carefully. After giving it a thorough examination, she handed it back.

"No," she said.

"That's one of Dan's cuff links in it."

She scowled.

"I wouldn't know about that," she said, "but I do know about the shirt. It isn't Dan's."

"How do you know? How can you be so sure?"

"He never wears any dress-up stuff like that."

"Gold cuff links are dress-up stuff."

"I've never seen him wear them."

The inspector picked that up.

"And you've never seen him wear this shirt or one like it," he said. "Isn't that all you can really tell me about it? How could you know he doesn't own a shirt like this and he's just never worn it for you to see?"

She was so ready with her answer that her reply all but clipped off the inspector's closing words.

"If Dan ever had a dress-up shirt, it wouldn't be this kind of rag," she explained. "This thing is fancy, but it's crappy fancy. The material is cheap junk, and the sewing is terrible. It'll come apart at the seams before you've had it a month. I know how Dan is about the stuff he buys. He wants quality. He wants it to wear a long time."

The argument seemed specious. The inspector had a try at knocking it down.

"He buys quality," he said. "He knows quality. He knows it in jeans and T-shirts and sweaters, the things he customarily buys. Now this is something else again. How do you know he didn't get taken when he bought this?"

"He's no fool," she said. "Just looking at it, he'd know it was no good. Look at the label. Made in Taiwan. Dan won't touch anything made in Taiwan. It's against his principles. I've been in the supermarket with him. Just a little shopping takes him forever because on any label he has to read every last bit of the fine print. Nothing from Taiwan, nothing from Chile, nothing from South Africa."

She picked up the jeans and subjected them to a similar examination. When she handed them to the inspector, she seemed a shade less certain of herself. Now she was volunteering nothing.

"What about the jeans?" Schmitty asked.

"They're the best jeans you can buy," she answered.

"Dan's?"

She reached up and took Mallard's hand, pulling his arm even tighter around her.

"Yes," she said, mustering no more than a frightened whisper. "They are Dan's."

It seemed to me that would be the admission he wanted, but the inspector wasn't satisfied with it.

"Because they're good quality?" he asked. "They could be his or they are his?"

"They are his. I mended them for him where he snagged them on a nail. I know my own sewing."

"Thanks," the inspector said. "Now about you? You all went out together—you, Dan, the kids. He brought the kids home, but you didn't come back until later. We'll need to know where you went and what you did."

She started to answer; but, stopping her, Mallard spoke for her.

"No," he said. "No way. I don't know what goes on. It's something crazy and it looks like it's something that involves me. Whatever it is, and I don't know what, this much I do know. It doesn't involve Norah. She doesn't have to answer any questions about herself or what she did or does or will do."

She made a move to draw away from him a bit. She didn't get far with it. His arm was still around her and he drew her back in close.

"It's all right, Danny," she said. "I don't mind. I want to answer. There's no reason why not." She turned to us. "I went shopping," she said, breaking out a smile. It was a forced smile if I've ever seen one. "It's something every woman does before she gets married."

"No parcels," the inspector said. "Have everything sent?"

"I didn't buy anything. Everything I saw was too expensive."

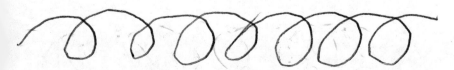

It was reasonable. There was no way anyone could have picked a hole in it, but it was unconvincing. There was something in the look of her and in the sound of the way she was pushing her statements at the inspector that made it difficult, if not impossible, to believe her. Just moments earlier her tone had been different. When she'd been talking about the Taiwan label and about knowing her own sewing, it had been difficult not to believe in her.

Mallard created a diversion. He went into an act, assuming the good-provider role.

"Look, baby," he said. "If there's anything you want, we've got the money. It's a time for being extravagant."

"I couldn't do it," she told him. "It'd make me sick. I don't think I could ever learn."

Between the two of them, they put on a good performance of having become so deeply involved one with the other that they had forgotten we were there. We can perform as well. Inspector Schmidt gave me the sign and we tiptoed out without so much as a "see you later."

I waited till we were out of earshot.

"I can't see where that got you much," I said.

"We could have done worse. It's all fitting together."

"Fitting together with what?"

"Motherhood, mugging, murder, masquerade, and marriage."

"Alliteration," I said. "May I remind you of where that got Spiro Agnew?"

"It wasn't the alliteration that did it. So if you can take one more M, there's another move to come."

"And you're happy about the whole thing?"

"Another move to come, and for this one we can lay a trap."

"Entrapment?"

"Of course not. Nothing more than watchful waiting.

Our man is going to make his move. He won't need a push."

We were galloping along as we talked. Inspector Schmidt had that urgency that I have long since learned to take as a signal that he has all the answers and is ready to close in.

We zipped around to precinct where he told Wishes Leary what he wanted done. He wanted Hazel picked up and held.

"Okay," Wishes said. "On what charge?"

"Material witness. Take her in for her own protection and take her in without anybody knowing. We don't want her bumped off before she can testify."

"That one," I said. "You'll never get her to testify."

"I can pretend to be stupid enough to think it's worth a try, can't I?" Schmitty said. He turned back to Leary. "We'll need a bit of a special setup for it," he said. "We don't want to take her out of her flat, and we don't want to pick her up anywhere that any of the neighbors can see it. We don't want the word to get around."

"Now wait a minute," Leary said. "I've got to live with these people. I need at least a few friends in this precinct. I start playing it sneaky and I won't have any."

The inspector was set for full speed ahead. He was hearing no objections.

"I'm watching it," he said. "We're okay. She's a witness but a reluctant one. Reluctant witnesses who say too much without saying enough are the kind of witnesses we lose because someone gets to them and bumps them off. We have to protect her, and nobody can fault us for doing it in a way that is safest for her. Nobody will know we have her. So when someone wants to go after her, he won't know where to go. It's perfectly legal and perfectly prudent. Relax, Wishes, relax."

Leary trusted him. I must admit that in his place I would

have had my doubts, even though I should have known better. They put their heads together and worked out their method. She had a telephone. Although she transacted much of her business in her ground-floor front, that was for trade she might lure in from the street. She also went out on call.

Wishes supplied that information. The inspector was delighted with it. It made things beautifully easy. Wishes had the phone number. The inspector dialed it and Schmitty was so convincingly the john from Keokuk in town on business, and too horny to wait until dark, that it was only because I know him so well that I didn't believe he was about to take time out from the chase to work in a quickie.

He set it up for her to come to him. He said just as soon as she could make it. He would be waiting. He gave her an address at the edge of the precinct where some abandoned slaughterhouses, which hadn't been using their river view, had been torn down, and an island of luxury housing had been intruded into the surrounding slums.

His call completed, he hung up.

"She says to give her a half hour," he said. "So we have fifteen minutes to stake it out. I want her picked up down there, just before she goes into the building."

A couple of men out of the precinct detective squad handled it. We waited in the station house with Leary until they'd brought her in.

"How long do you think you can hold her?" I asked.

"More than long enough," the inspector said. "If we haven't buttoned the whole thing up before morning, we'll never get it licked."

He was heading for the street. I tagged after him. He had me confused.

"You've got her," I said. "She's going to take a lot of

breaking down. She won't talk just for the asking. Aren't you even going to make a start on questioning her?"

"Wouldn't do any good," the inspector said, and went on walking. He was so much in a hurry that it was more like running.

"It just might." I'd had a thought. "She was on her way to a dumb yokel she had every reason to believe would be good for more than the going rate. It must have looked like a great assignment, one she'd hate to miss. For that matter, missing any assignment is bad for business. She wouldn't want the word to get around in salesman circles that she made a promise and then never turned up. If you try her now, she might just tell you everything she knows in the hope that she could still make it and not be too late for that most promising assignation."

"She has nothing to tell," the inspector said. "She knows nothing. She started out by telling more than she knows. She took off from nothing more solid than envy and malice. I needed her out of the way. So now forget her. She's out of the way."

"Out of the way of what?" I asked.

"Out of the way of our using her flat."

"To stake out the building? But why all this? You have Blau's flat. Why don't we use that?"

"Because we're not looking for anything that'll happen under the stairs outside Blau's door. The action is going to be up above."

We galloped around to Dinah's and picked up a load of take-out food. Obviously we were holing up for what Schmitty might have been expecting would be a long vigil. At the house, Inspector Schmidt did a loid job on Hazel's lock. He had us inside the place faster than you could have done it with a key.

"She's just the type to take this as a heaven-sent opportunity to raise hell," I said.

"No way she'll ever know."

"On that kind of thinking, a lot of people are in jail."

The inspector laughed that comment off.

Joined by two of Wishes Leary's precinct men, we waited and we watched. We saw Norah and Dan go out. They had all the kids with them. We let them go. The inspector had that covered. He had set it up with Leary. A two-man tail picked them up and stayed with them all the time they were out. If they separated, there would be a man on each. It hadn't seemed necessary to have any separate cover for the kids.

Inspector Schmidt could take his chances on them.

XI.

We ate. We got that out of the way early because we had to take turns at it, one keeping a window watch while the others fed. Furthermore, the inspector wanted the eating done before dark would set in. We couldn't allow ourselves any lights.

When night had come and we were waiting and watching in the dark, it came to be steadily more and more like being the subject of a sensory-deprivation experiment. It was not only a matter of no lights. It was also no sound. We were sure we had managed to slip into Hazel's place without anyone seeing us. The inspector was bent on keeping it that way. He was taking not even the slightest chance of anyone hearing us.

Throughout the evening the silence in which we waited was only our own. All manner of sounds came at us from outside, street sounds, sounds of revelry from the flats over our heads. Norah and Dan, home again with the kids, seemed to be in a gay and carefree mood. I suspected that it had to be forced gaiety, each one putting it on past fear and worry but putting it on for the other's benefit. I wanted to think it was that and not their putting it on for our benefit. I saw no way that they could have known that we were down in the flat below them, but I also could see no way that they could genuinely be as carefree as they sounded.

We heard them getting the boys to bed. The process seemed to be mixed up with a lot of hilarious fooling. It

was late for the kids before all that had quieted down, but somewhere close to eleven it stopped and after that the silence was only occasionally broken. We could guess that Norah and Dan were still up. Now and again we heard footsteps. This would be their chance for talking seriously, now that the boys were all asleep. I wondered whether they were talking about the future, planning the life that lay ahead of them, or whether they had other more pressing things to work out together, like trying to guess how much the inspector knew and trying to plan what their next move should be and how they should make it.

Shortly after one o'clock, a woman who lived alone on the third floor came in with a man. He was a little drunk. They went past our door and on up the stairs, stumbling a little as they went and giggling a lot. Another fifteen-minute interval of silence and then just over our heads the baby cried. It was easy to picture that. It would be little Danny wet again. I wondered which of them would be changing him.

The next hour and more was the complete drag, no sound, no movement, only the lights of the occasional car that passed in the street, only the hiss of its tires on the pavement.

It was shortly after three when he came. There was not enough light out in the street for a face to register as anything more than a whitish blur with features insufficiently articulated for recognition. Since he was wearing a broad-brimmed hat, his face, furthermore, was shadowed, catching not even the minor glow shed by the streetlights.

I hadn't known for whom we were watching. I hadn't even known that the event for which we had been waiting would be coming by way of the street. Although I had been there side by side with Inspector Schmidt keeping the watch, I had perhaps been even more intent on listening,

more than half expecting that, whatever it was to be, it would begin in one of the flats above our heads.

The moment he came into sight, however, I knew, and it was my own independent knowing. It wasn't that I was cued in by any feeling that the inspector was tensing up beside me. It was the man's walk and his bearing that made him immediately recognizable. You might think that he wouldn't be the only man in the world or even the only man in the city who had it, but it was too wildly unlikely that another would be coming to that place on that night at that hour.

The inspector didn't wait for him to reach the stretch of street immediately in front of the house.

"I'm going upstairs," he whispered to one of the precinct men. "I'll be on the stairs between the second and third. I can come down on him from there. You be ready to cut him off from below. We don't move until he's committed himself. We want to get him in the act."

He was taking the other of Leary's men with him. I was to remain down below. I was wondering what act he was expecting. Was it to be Norah this time or Dan? If he found them together, I could imagine that it might be both.

The inspector and the man he was taking upstairs with him slipped away in the dark; and I was alone with the remaining precinct cop to watch the guy make his approach to the house. As he came closer, I could see that he was carrying something. It was too big and too bulky. I could make no sense of it, not in terms of the weapons he had previously used or in terms of any imaginable new weapon he might have taken up.

To dispose of Eddie Blue, it had been his fists and the length of pipe. For Henrietta Blau, it had been nothing he had brought with him. Then it had been a quick improvisation with the electric cord that just happened to have been

ready to hand. For me, it had been the pail of suds, again an improvisation with what he'd had handy.

Now it was a bulky package, obviously no container for a knife or a gun and equally wrong for a length of pipe or a stretch of electric cord. The package could easily have contained a pail, but that was too silly. For want of anything else available in his moment of need, a killer might pick up a pail and use it to beat someone's head in, but it was just not conceivable that, coming as he was now, he would be bringing it with him as his weapon of choice.

I had a few moments of thinking that the inspector had been making a great leap in the dark and that he was now landing nowhere. I couldn't keep the thought. The pattern was fitting together too neatly and, now that I was finally seeing it, I could understand how Inspector Schmidt had come to it before me. There was only the one contradictory element and it was the strange package the man was carrying.

He reached the house and he came right in, moving smoothly and silently. We switched to the door and opened it a crack so we could watch him from there and move in easily behind him as soon as he had started up the stairs. Seeing the way he was stealing into the building erased for me any lingering doubt I might have had of the inspector's reasoning.

I was even coming up with an explanation of his package. I thought it might be a nastily malicious joke—a wedding present for Norah and Dan he would leave to be found with their bodies. All the pieces were fitting together for me. He was the other half of the two-man team and, because he had been in it, Norah had gone so long as the only welfare mother in the house who hadn't been touched.

It had been too long. People had begun to talk and to think and to wonder. I could see where Norah, herself,

would have been wondering and might have begun asking questions. There had been only the one way to knock off such dangerous speculations. Norah had to have her turn, but the guy loved her. He couldn't bring himself to do any part of it. So for this one, Blue had worked alone and Blue had gone too far. Maybe it was because Blue had been like that, and for this one on which he had been on his own, there had been no control. More likely it had been because Norah fought him, and Blue was too clumsy and too stupid to handle that without carrying the violence too far.

Either way, what had been planned as a move toward safety had opened fresh dangers. Norah had known who her assailant was and what she had begun to suspect would have now been confirmed for her. She had known that her man, the father of her sons, had been working some kind of a connection with Eddie Blue and now she knew what it was.

The fact that her man had pulled away from the attack on her, that he had been unable to raise his own hand toward doing her harm would for her have been no consolation and no palliative to his betrayal. He had walked away from it and had left her to the mercies of Eddie Blue.

When he had visited her in the hospital, she had told him that she was through with him, but at that stage he would have been thinking of ways he could take to go about winning her back.

His first move would be to avenge on Eddie Blue the injuries Blue had inflicted on her. Evidently this was a character so versatile that he had a talent for burglary as well as for mugging. He had keys. They might have been individual keys or a master. That was a detail that made no difference. I didn't have to speculate about the keys.

Now, as I watched through the door crack, I was seeing him do something that wasn't in the pattern as I had come

to see it. It was to be out of pattern for the inspector's expectations as well. The man didn't head for the stairs. He went on past them and with a key he let himself into the flat at the ground-floor rear, the place where Henrietta Blau had lived and where the night before he had murdered the old woman. He shut and locked the door behind him.

I tried to fit that move into the scenario. It was crazy, but it might explain his package. As he had gone back to Blue's flat to try to clear away the evidence that would fix it as the scene of that murder, could he now be in that ground-floor rear scrubbing away at what he thought might be evidence that could identify him as the man who had done the second killing? It seemed absurdly late for any such attempt, but I could think of nothing else he could be doing behind that door he had locked after him.

On that I was still speculating, but the rest of it was clear. We had seen him go back into the hospital after our visit to Norah. She must have told him then that she was not giving him away. She had told the inspector nothing. She couldn't bring herself to hand him over to the police. She had loved the man, and he was the father of her boys. He had nothing to fear from her, but he also could hope for nothing from her. She was through with him.

He would have gone away from there bent on winning her back. He went to her place and picked up her ID card. He needed that to make certain that, when Blue's body was found, she would know beyond any doubt that Blue was the man who had mugged her and that for that he had been killed.

Can't you imagine it?

"I love you, baby. See how much I love you. I got even with him for what he did to you."

He was sure he could count on Norah's silence, but now he had run himself into the problem of Henrietta Blau. He

had to silence her. Henrietta knew he would be coming and she thought she could deal with him. She had the old flatiron ready. It was to be her defensive armament. Menacing him with it, she would hold him off while she convinced him that he could let her go on living. Her silence could be bought.

She had been waiting for him when the inspector and I turned up. She had known he was in the building, and the noisy performance she had put on with us had been for his benefit. It had warned him off until she had been rid of us. She hadn't wanted the law to have him for the murder of her son. Her son was gone and with him the source of additional income—her share of the take in the muggings. Justice would bring her no profit. Blackmail would be more to her advantage.

You can figure for yourself how it would have seemed to her. Luck had brought her what should have been the perfect setup for her talk with her son's killer. She'd have the inspector and me ready to hand in Mallard's place directly above her. She was counting on the man doing nothing hasty while the law was hovering that close to him. You know that she miscalculated, but you can understand how safe she would have been feeling.

So there he was. He had murdered twice and Norah was still not coming back to him. I suppose that was something he could never understand. He was the great sex machine, and he couldn't believe that he could have lost her because of nothing more than her being irreparably revolted by what she had otherwise found him to be. He thought there had to be more reason than that. Looking for something more, he'd hit on Dan Mallard.

It had to be Mallard. Mallard was winning her away from him. That started the guy on a new program. Get Mallard. He recognized that sooner or later the police

would find the place where Blue had been living. If he could get there before them, he would take the precaution of doing a clean-up just in case they might be able to bring up fingerprints on the length of pipe. At the same time he would fix Mallard.

He had the keys. A small spot of burglary in Mallard's flat and he had the cuff link, the one thing he could find that would be an unmistakable clue to Mallard. He dropped the cuff link for the police to find, and he was scrubbing up when we came along. We had him trapped and he had to get himself out of that. You already know how he managed it.

In the doing, however, he came up with the idea for a further improvisation. He could cinch the evidence against Mallard. He bought the cheap shirt with the french cuffs. Returning to Mallard's place, he put the second cuff link into the shirt he'd bought, took from Mallard's closet a pair of Dan's jeans and a pair of his sandals, soaked the lot in that stinking detergent, and left the mess for Inspector Schmidt to find when he would come down on Mallard about the cuff link.

Of course, he'd been misjudging Norah all the way. He had also been misjudging Mallard. Mallard knew about him. He couldn't not have known, and he'd told the inspector nothing. There was only one possible reason for Mallard's silence. For the big guy, Norah and the little boys came first. He would do nothing that could in any way hurt them. There had been no way Norah or he could have known what the cuff links and the detergent-soaked shirt meant, but they knew that the inspector had the one cuff link; and there was no way they couldn't guess that it was all in some way connected with an effort to frame Mallard for the killings.

They still had said nothing. I could see where she would

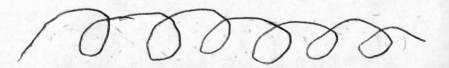

think the frame couldn't possibly be made to stick; and as a last resort, if it did begin to look as though the frame might hold up, she could always talk. Meanwhile Mallard was not going to talk unless she did.

When she had let Dan take the boys home and had gone off by herself, she hadn't been shopping. She had been to see the killer. She had told him that if he hadn't believed she was through with him, he might be convinced now. She was marrying Mallard, and he was to lay off. One more move to hurt this man who would in a few days be her husband, and all bets would be off. She would go to the inspector and tell him everything she knew. She knew more than enough to hang the man and he was fully aware of it.

Coming home from that, she was confronted with the cuff link and detergent business. Since it was obvious that all that had been done before the talk she had just previously had with the killer, it would have seemed to her that it added nothing. Since the doing of it had preceded her last warning to the killer and had not followed it, she still kept silent.

Being the woman she was, it was the only thing she could have done. That, however, doesn't change the fact that she couldn't have made a worse choice of how she was to handle the situation. He had killed twice in his effort not to lose her. If he was now to lose her in any case, he was not the character to allow it to stand as it was. He was not going to hold still for losing her to another man. He was past the place where another murder mattered. It could be the one more—Dan Mallard; but then it would have to be two more—both Mallard and Norah.

So now he was in the flat below them, doing some crazy job of clean-up. I thought I could understand that. If he thought it was necessary, it would have to be done before

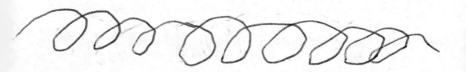

he went upstairs to do his killings. After those, he would want to be quickly away.

We held our station, watching the closed door and waiting for him to come out and start up the stairs. It threw us off completely when the silence was broken and it was Inspector Schmidt who shattered it. He came thundering down the stairs. We jumped out to meet him.

"Smoke," he was shouting. "Fire. Where is he?"

I jerked a thumb toward the ground-floor rear.

The inspector charged past the precinct man and me and headed back there. We followed after him. We were about to hit the door when it slammed open. Our man was in the doorway coming right at us, and behind him the flat that had been Henrietta Blau's roared up in flame. Seeing us, he jumped back and slammed the door against us. We couldn't go after him. We needed the few moments during which that closed door might hold back the flames from exploding into the hall and shooting up the stairwell. On every one of the upper floors there were people asleep.

Even to the last I had underestimated the man's savagery. For that matter, the inspector hadn't foreseen this either. Another murder or even two more murders had been conceivable, but this had been beyond imagining. To get the woman he felt had betrayed him and the man who had taken her away from him, he had been ready to take along with their lives the lives of his own sons and the lives of all the other people asleep in that building.

I dived for the stairs and for once the inspector wasn't a step ahead of me. We went up side by side, shouting as we went. He took one door and I the other. The precinct lads charged on up to take the next floor above. Floor by floor we roused the whole house.

All the time I was thinking that someone should be turning in the fire alarm, but we had no time for it. We were at

the top of the house with the people from the upper floors gathered around us, when we heard the fire engines. We learned later that Mallard had taken care of that. Too excited to sleep, he had been the first to hear and comprehend the inspector's shout. While Norah had been getting the kids up, he'd hit his telephone and called in the alarm. Then he had helped her get her brood down the stairs and out of the building, herding them out to the street even in that moment when the fire came through the wood of that closed door to envelop the hall behind them and go roaring up the stairwell.

With the people we had around us at the top of the house, we made it out to the roof. The fire was funneling up the stairs. Smoke was making the roof impossible. Together we shepherded the people from roof to roof, herding them over to the building next door. There the firemen met us on the stairs. They took over on the evacuation.

Behind the fire lines out in the street, we caught up with Norah and Dan. The inspector flung it at her straight.

"It didn't just catch fire," he said. "It was set on fire and you know who did it. He was in there when we last saw him. If he got out, you . . . "

She wasn't waiting for him to finish.

"If he got out," she said, "I'll take you to him. I'll find him wherever he goes. He won't be able to get away from me. He would have killed my babies. The one wasn't enough for him."

She didn't have to help the inspector find him. When they'd brought the fire under control, the firemen turned up what was left of him. Dodging away from us, he had plowed through flame to the windows and there he had died. Those ground-floor windows were fitted with iron bars. Designed to keep the like of him from coming in

through the windows, the bars had served to hold him inside the burning flat.

It was a bad moment when they brought the body out. It
hit Norah hard. Shutting her eyes against it, she turned to
Dan. Putting his arms around her, he held her close and
buried her face in the crook of his shoulder. It was, however, only for a moment. Norah stiffened and pulled away
from him.

"We've got to forget all of this," Dan said. "Forget him.
Forget the lot."

"No Dan," she said. "Not possible, Dan. I have too
many reminders. He was the father of my boys."

"That's just biology," Dan said. "They were yours. They
were never his. Possession cannot come except with love.
They are ours—yours, Norah, and mine."

"Yes," she said. "I know. They are, but still . . . "

"You want to put the wedding off? Wait a while? I've
waited. I can wait some more."

"No," she said. "We won't wait. He's the past and that's
where I must keep him."

So they were married on schedule, and it was a great
day. Dinah outdid herself. There were no tears. If, when
the time came for tossing the rice, things got unconvention-
ally moist, it was only because for that occasion the little
boys had water in their pistols.

It was Inspector Schmidt's contribution to the festivities.